FORBIDDEN BLOSSOM

NOLA LI BARR

Tapioca Press

Edited by Qat Wanders

Cover design by Rob Williams

Library of Congress Control Number: 2018913679

ISBN 978-1-7327814-0-5 (paperback)

ISBN 978-1-7327814-1-2 (ebook)

www.nolalibarr.com

First Edition

❀ Created with Vellum

For Gordon Barr

I

THE VALLEY STRETCHED until it met the waterfall where it fell down a cascade of rocks into the pool in front of me. I sank my toes into the water's edge and let the cool liquid kiss me gently as I said goodbye. We had been hiking this trail following the water, and I never got tired of it. This is where I would come to reset when I needed a break from reality.

"We better be going," said Victoria. She and I had been visiting California for the last month. We had tried to hit every tourist stop and attraction we could find. After all, what's the point of a road trip if you didn't stop? My favorite thing to do was to find nature, sit, and listen. If you were really quiet, you would hear the water, the trees, the insects, the squirrels digging in the ground looking for food, the birds flying in between the limbs, and the sounds of foliage rustling as larger animals traversed to their next destination. I loved the idea of moving from place to place. I loved it so much I didn't have a place I called home.

My first job after college lasted about two years before I gave it up to drive around the US and explore my home country. In order to keep my mom and Victoria updated, I taught myself HTML and created my own website. My blog started catching the eyes of some sponsors who allowed me to do what I do. Travel blog around the world. However, this weekend was my mother's birthday, and I was going to surprise her by showing up at her home with some postcards I had collected. She loved them and would put them around her condo to show off to her friends all the places her daughter had traveled. My mom was who started me on this travel kick. Every year, we would plan a big trip, just the two of us, to some far-off destination. She painted professionally and would close the shop for two weeks, so we could go have our adventure.

Nowadays, my mom didn't go anywhere. She said her body was getting old, and she didn't move so easily, but I still hoped to bring her with me on this next trip. I was planning a visit to Taiwan, her mom's home country, and I wanted her to come. She had been once as a little girl and the stories she told still resonated with me. Exotic food, sauces her mom hadn't even made, and the open markets were fascinating. I wanted to see them all, but I'd been avoiding Taiwan because it seemed like sacred ground. It was a place I needed my mom with me. We would go on a pilgrimage. If only I could convince her.

"Well, if you're done meditating over there, let's get a move on. The sun will set soon, and I'd like to get back for a shower," said Victoria while walking away.

"I'm coming." I grabbed my bag and followed behind. At least it wasn't a long flight. Mom lived in Astoria, Oregon. A short jump to the next state.

"Mom! I'm home," as I opened the front door to reveal a hallway covered in pictures from when I was an infant all the way to the present. I could smell marinated meat wafting from the kitchen and it pulled me in like a long-lost friend. "I hope it's okay, but I invited Victoria to come too."

There was a blur of a woman and the next thing I knew I was in the arms of Mom giving me a big 'ol bear hug. She smelled like clean laundry—probably ocean breeze. It was really nice to be back.

"You're home! This is the best surprise! Have you forgotten all about that boy on your trip through California?" Mom asked with expectant eyes. I could see her trying to read me.

"Mom, it's not that easy. Brian and I were together for four years. You don't just forget someone like that. But yes, Victoria and I had a great time, and I didn't think about him most of the time."

"Well, that's a start," as she let me go and reached for Victoria. "Victoria, oh, it's so good to see you again. The last time you came was probably when you were all graduating high school."

"That sounds about right, but I couldn't say no to some home cooking when I'm invited," Victoria teased, giving Mom an equally big hug.

Victoria and I had known each other since high school. She had moved to Astoria our freshman year, and we bonded over our mutual no-friends status. We ended up spending the rest of high school together joined at the hip and took all the same classes. The only difference was Victoria had long auburn hair that shined when she let it all down. She wore tight-fitting clothes, but never too short, and knew how to hold up her end of a conversation. Her makeup was flawless and sometimes her beauty would extend even to the tip of her nails. She was super sophisticated compared to me.

By the time we had graduated from high school Victoria had dated three guys with more waiting. I was American Born Chinese (otherwise known as ABC) and had the standard black hair, which I always kept up in a ponytail. My eyelids folded in so no amount of mascara would ever make my eyes look big or my eyelashes long. Lipstick barely made my thin lips stand out. The sight of a boy made me freeze up, but I was *really* good at school. Tutoring two boys was about as close to a date as I ever got.

Then, Brian showed up at college. Brian was also ABC, standard buzz cut, cute dimples, and Mom liked him because he could speak Chinese. Not that her English wasn't perfect as she was born and raised here too, but she thought it important that someone who looked Chinese should still know how to speak the language.

Four blissful years followed. I studied engineering, had a boyfriend, had my best friend, and was living the life at the college away from my parents. We all managed to graduate, and then I found out he never saw us in a serious relationship. Our relationship was apparently just a fling for him and other girls were attracting his attention. A four-year fling. He moved on to a big sales role with Google in San Francisco and last I heard had another girlfriend already. Victoria found a job in San Antonio and I moved to New York. We couldn't haven't scattered further apart unless we left the country, but Victoria and I made a commitment to meet up every six months in a different city and hence began my love for road trips. I called it quits after two years on-the-job testing new machinery, making PowerPoint slides, presenting my findings, and then repeating. The travel bug was more enticing than the minute dimensions of a cubicle. So here I was. Traveling with no signs of stopping. What I didn't know was that six months earlier someone decided my life was due for a change.

SIX MONTHS EARLIER IN PORTLAND

"Sir, Sir, wake up, wake up! You were having a nightmare again."

I slowly opened my eyes and looked around me. My pillow was damp from the tears in my eyes, and I was in the same four-poster bed I had slept in for the last 60+ years. These days, it was where I spent the majority of my time. The curtains were open, and the sun was shining in. Andy had opened the window just a bit to let some snowy fresh air come in. It rarely snowed here, but when it did, I was at my happiest.

The dream was still vivid in my head. Her looking back one last time trying not to cry. My father's hand holding onto my shoulders as I shook with fury while trying to hold back tears. Trying with all my might to be brave for her. The scene kept replaying in my mind, and I knew what I had to do.

"Andy, please get Sebastian on the phone."

"Yes, sir. Should I ask him to come over?"

"Yes, that would be a good idea, and is the trunk in good shape?"

"Yes, sir. I had it dusted, and the lock has been re-oiled."

"Thank you, Andy. I don't know what I would do without you."

Sally and I never had kids which was just as well. I only hope it wasn't too late to make amends.

2

WE THREW the best party for Mom. Her friends joined us for a morning brunch, we decorated her whole house, and we sang and danced until she and her friends fell asleep in the living room. Victoria and I left shortly after. Last night, Victoria had mentioned she was going to take a break from work as well and go traverse Europe to see if she could figure out what she wanted to do with her life. She had seen me doing it for a couple of years now, and she wanted to give it a try. I fully encouraged her, and we decided today was going to be our last hurrah before we went our separate ways for a while. We sat at our favorite spot: side table for two at the local Market Cafe. Small red awning over us to block the sun, and the perfect place to people-watch. We were leaning back, reminiscing on memories, and breathing in the snowy air.

I had put on my favorite outfit of skinny jeans, button-down flannel, ankle-high boots, long leaf earrings, beanie hat, and my favorite burnt orange and white scarf. Today was going to be a good day, and I wouldn't think otherwise. Victoria was a friend who always came back. Some would call her a true friend. I called her my only friend. Besides Victoria, Brian, and my mom, I didn't really hang out with anyone. All of my other friends lived abroad in the places I had temporarily lived, and the others were Brian's, and they went back to him as soon as we broke up. It was like I never existed in their lives. At first, it hurt, but then I realized I liked being by myself a lot more. Being able to make my own decisions and do whatever I wanted when I wanted to do it. Plus, social media helped because I could control when and where I wanted to socialize.

On the way out the door, I had grabbed an overnight envelope that must have been delivered when we were dancing.

"Aren't you going to open it?" asked Victoria while ogling the boys walking by.

"I feel kind of guilty leaving my mom this morning. Maybe we shouldn't stay here too long."

"You always feel guilty when you come home. Your mom hasn't left the house in years. Remember, Asian guilt. You try too hard to be the perfect daughter."

"You always say that. You could do with more love toward your mom. I feel like I'm the only excitement in her life these days and I should stick around and keep her company. Plus, I'm not staying for too long. I really want to go check out Taiwan and I might have a chance to write about the yummy food there."

"My mom and I have a certain type of relationship we have both agreed upon, and it works for the both of us. I show her I love her in my own way, sometimes via postcards, but at least I keep in touch."

"Anyway, you better ask one of those boys out before you drool all over your shirt," I said while tearing the package open.

"I should ask one of them out for you before you forget that being alone is not the way to live."

"I'm not ready yet," I said while staring at what I had just pulled out of the package.

"What did you get? You look like you forgot what you were doing."

"Um . . . I'm not sure. It doesn't make sense."

"Let me see it," as she tore the paper out of my hands.

. . .

Dear Anne Huang,

As you might have read in the news, Sir Anthony Wilkens passed away six months ago. Sir Anthony named you as a beneficiary in the will, for which I am the executor. We have successfully finished the probate and request your presence at the reading of the will on Tuesday, November 16, 2010, at 3:00 p.m.

4663 Main St., Portland, OR

Please call 555-256-7766 to confirm receipt of this letter, and I look forward to meeting you.

Sincerely,

Sebastian Gole

"Wow," said Victoria as her mouth went from an O to a laugh so loud the other customers turned to stare.

"This is not funny. There must be a mistake."

"You're going to become some rich heiress and be able to travel the world in style now!" she almost fell out of her seat from laughing so hard.

"Why couldn't that happen?" I glared at her.

"Sorry, you, navigating that type of world just seems impossible."

"Some friend you are. Plus, it's probably just some old guy who wrote down the wrong name because he was too senile. I'll just give Sebastian a call."

"You don't know who Sir Anthony is, do you?"

"I've heard the name. He's a rich guy who lives up in the hills of Portland. He donated some computers to the local elementary one year."

"Yeah . . . I'll just let you find out for yourself. Why don't you call him right now?"

"Fine, I will." I made a point of pulling out my phone, punching in the number, and putting the phone to my ear. It had hardly finished ringing once when a sweet voice flowed from the phone.

"Schuster and Schuster Law Firm. How may we help you?"

"Hi. I got a letter today saying I was named one of the beneficiaries of Sir Anthony Wilkens. I think there is a mistake as I have no relations . . ."

"Please hold."

"This is Sebastian Gole. With whom am I speaking?" His voice sounded so much like Brian's. Low, confident. Images of jet black hair, soft lips, piercing black eyes that made my legs wobble when he looked at me, hands that were soft and left lingering caresses on me . .
.

"Hello? I'm very busy so . . ."

"Sorry, yes, this is Anne, I received—um—" wow, my mind had gone blank, "right, a letter from you today saying I was named one of the beneficiaries of Sir Anthony Wilkens. I think there has been a mistake, and I wanted to let you know."

"No, there isn't a mistake. You are on the list. Anne Hong-Mei Huang right? You are the daughter of Josephine He-Mei Lin and granddaughter of Rose En-Hui Chen?"

"Yes . . . how do you know all this?"

"Because it's all in the will. I'll see you tomorrow at 3 o'clock. Looking forward to meeting you."

"I—" but he had already hung up. Very rude, but I was too shocked to think of a good comeback. Plus, he had already hung up.

"Well, looks like you're going to a will-reading whether you like to or not."

"I don't have to go."

"Go! I want to know what you are a beneficiary of. Please."

"Okay, okay. It's not that I'm not curious. If it is a lot of money, my mom could come and travel with me to our hearts' content. I could paint, take pictures, open a flower store—anything I wanted."

Victoria came over and put an arm around me. "I know we were both looking forward to living at your mom's place for a bit, visiting nightclubs, meeting cute boys, planning your next adventure to an exotic location filled with—"

"Stop it! I said I was going," trying not to laugh too hard.

"Good, because I seriously can't think of you doing any of those things except for the next adventure part. Glad I didn't have to come save you."

I threw my napkin at her. Victoria was never good at masking what she thought, and she knew me too well. I felt happy that I had such a good friend. We ordered our favorite lattes and croissants and gorged on them until we were full. Then we went for a walk around the city and window-shopped.

3

VICTORIA and I came home around three in the morning. She found my keys in my purse and dragged me into my room where she plopped me onto my bed. This is where I found myself the next morning. The sound of my mother clanging dishes in the kitchen woke me from my drowsiness, and I made myself sit up and concentrate on getting out of bed. I went to the bathroom and washed my face and was startled at how puffy my eyelids were. The eyelashes folded so far into the lids I already looked like I had no definition there. Now they were swollen, and I looked like a puffer fish. Nothing I could do about it now.

"Well, there's my sleepy head. Last night must have been tremendous fun for you two," she said with a side look at me.

"If you're suggesting we hooked up with someone, you are wrong. We went dancing, and yes, I drank too much. Is Victoria still here?"

"She went to visit her parents. Said she'd call you before she headed out. I made you some congee."

"Mmm, thanks, Mom. It smells delicious."

"I had a lovely birthday yesterday. You were the best present a mom could get. I can't keep up with all the places you go to now."

I loved my mom. She was hard on me growing up, but unlike

other Asian parents, she supported me no matter what decision I made. She never got mad when I told her I left engineering to go travel, but actually seemed jealous and sent me care packages while I was on the road. Some of my Chinese classmates growing up were first-generation Americans and most are still an engineer, a medical doctor, or a lawyer. Making the big bucks, buying the big house and fancy cars, and living the American dream. That is why their parents came here in the first place, so I can't blame them. Mom didn't even give me a hard time on getting married and producing grandbabies. I sometimes thought this was because she was also born in the United States—so she gave me more slack. Her childhood might have been harder because her parents were new to America, but she rarely talked about her parents. My memories of my mom's mom, my Ai Po, were vague and probably stemmed more from pictures. Mom said I had visited her twice, but I can't remember those visits except that there was a distinct mothball smell around her.

"Mom, I got this letter yesterday asking me to attend a will-reading today at 3:00 in Portland."

"Really, did you do some helpful deed to some family on one of your travels?"

"Not that I can think of. Not anyone that would have something to give me. I thought it was sent to the wrong family, but I called them and they said it was correct. Can you make heads or tails about it?"

"Who's the dead guy?"

"Nice, Mom. A Sir Anthony Wilkens."

At this, Mom went silent, took the letter, and started reading. She didn't say anything for a long time, and I was starting to wonder if she had zoned out. It wasn't that long of a letter. But then, in one motion, she handed me the letter and walked back to the kitchen.

"It looks official. I would go and see what they have to say. It might be something very important. You can always decline it if you don't want it. If you don't go, you'll always be curious why you were named a beneficiary."

"Do you know who Sir Anthony Wilkens is? Why would I be a beneficiary of his?"

"Sir Anthony Wilkens comes from a family that made their money from building things: railroad tracks, real estate, and stocks. I'm not sure Sir Anthony has ever really worked."

"Seriously? That brings me back to my question. Why would I be a beneficiary of his? And why aren't you as well?"

"You'll just have to find out. Don't tell me you are so comfortable that you aren't a bit excited about the possibility of inheriting a lot of money?"

"Of course I am, but it's just so weird. For all we know, he's giving out charity to everyone in town."

"Well, I live in the town." She finally had a smile back on her face.

"I know! I don't know. I'm a bit anxious and confused."

"Let me know how it goes. Now, eat your breakfast before it gets cold."

4

THE TWO-HOUR DRIVE to downtown Portland went by in a blur with my brain more focused on what I could be inheriting. My first stop was Powell's (a famous Portland-born bookstore) and I calmed when I breathed in the old- and new-book smells. My feet immediately took me to the travel section where I picked out some books on Taiwan. If I was going to persuade my mom to go with me I needed some ammunition, but I couldn't concentrate. I decided to walk to the reading and just wait there. Schuster and Schuster Law Firm radiated stuffiness and coldness from its glass and metal facade. Everyone coming in through the doors was dressed in nice suits and dresses that looked like they were tailored specifically for them from the finest materials in the world. Their hair and makeup were done up like they were going to a photo shoot. At least I had on a dress, tights, and boots instead of jeans and a t-shirt. I had even remembered to put earrings in again.

I held my head up high, walked through the door, and went up to the security desk to ask for Sebastian Gole where I was rerouted to the top floor—the 24th floor. When the elevator doors opened, I saw a floor to ceiling glass view of the entire city below me with Mount Hood in the background. It was staggering, and I felt like I was on top of the world. Mount Hood grounded me whenever I came back from my travels. It meant I was only a short two-hour drive home. Today was no different. The sight of it calmed me.

Sebastian's office was in the corner past a waiting area that was probably the size of my mom's house. The secretary sat at a desk immediately to the side of the door acting like a guardian you had to seek entrance from. All around me were cream wood walls polished to a gleam. The carpet was your usual dark blue office carpet tiles, but instead of one design repeated across the whole floor there were splotches of red, orange, and yellow dispersed with no pattern in mind. My only thought was they were trying too hard to appear hip. The doors had what looked like gold dragons around the handles. Maybe Sebastian was Chinese, but with a name like Gole that couldn't be possible. Maybe he was half Chinese on his mother's side. Now, I was curious.

I was one of the first few to arrive, and I settled myself in one of the armchairs. It was quite comfy, but I should have expected that from a place like this. Across from me was an older gentleman dressed in a light gray suit reading one of the free magazines on the table. He was slim and fit with a full head of light gray hair. As I sat down, he gave me a friendly smile with a curious look.

"Hello, I'm Jack" as he extended a hand out to me.

"I'm Anne. Nice to meet you."

"Are you here for Sir Anthony Wilken's will reading?"

"I am. I didn't realize I had to dress up for this."

"You didn't. I think you look quite nice. How did you know Anthony? I don't think I've ever met you at a family gathering."

"I don't know him. I actually don't know anything about him except what I found on the internet which was very slim on information. I got a letter that said I was a beneficiary and for me to come to this reading."

"Oh . . ." his eyes gleamed even brighter on hearing this.

"A word of advice. Don't let the others get to you."

Before I could ask him what he meant, we heard bustling coming from the elevators. A hoard of people were pushing their way out but still trying to look dignified. A woman younger than Jack came in first. She was in a white pantsuit, a pearl necklace and earrings, white heels, and everything in perfect placement down to the tip of her nails. Following her were what looked like her daughters, sons, and her children's spouses all dressed ready to attend a formal banquet. I watched Jack and the older woman exchange pleasantries, but then they sat down on opposite sides of the room, and no one talked. It was an eerie silence filled with extreme tension in the air. Everyone seemed to be holding their breath except for Jack and me. I could feel all eyes on me looking me up and down as if I was a weird specimen they had never seen before. Most were doing so with curiosity, but it made me squirm in my seat wondering how I had gotten there in the first place.

Next, came another entourage. This must be an older sibling. The woman was dressed clean and sharp in loose, tan pants with a bow tied at her waist and a pink silk top that flowed down her body to just below her waist. She had an air of confidence of someone used to leading the group, but she gave off a sense of serenity like she had come to terms with where she was in life. Her gray hair was the prettiest I'd ever seen. It shined radiantly, and every hair was placed perfectly around her head. There was a man holding her arm (I guessed him to be her husband), and they had their children and spouses trailing behind them. I thought they might be the last of the relatives when the most interesting sight came off the elevator.

This group was the loudest of them all and the most colorful. The eldest woman who was talking in a loud voice wore a multi-flower-print dress with a bright red belt around her waist, bright red three-inch heels, and bright red round earrings. Her hair had clearly been dyed a strawberry blonde, and she had so much makeup on I wondered if she had ever taken her makeup off since her 20s. Her husband wore green dress pants with a blue top, a straw dress hat, and the biggest smile I had seen on any of the people who had walked through this lobby. An entourage of their children followed behind them. They were all talking amongst themselves, but there were ten of them and you couldn't decipher who was talking to whom.

All the children looked like they were in their 50s, about my mother's age. I counted 25 people in the room with me, and that didn't include any of the grandkids or any potential great-grandkids. Also, all of these people were white, and they looked like they all knew each other. There went my theory that maybe Sir Anthony was going to give his money as a charity to a bunch of random people. Every attribute that made me Chinese started standing out like a sore spot in my mind. My heart was racing and I could feel my hands start to sweat. I didn't belong here. I grabbed onto the armchair to steady my hands and stared straight ahead at the plant in front of me in order to avoid staring at any particular person. I wished I could just sink into the wall. All twenty-four pairs of eyes were fixated on me. Only Jack was looking at everyone else. All of a sudden, he stood up, and my heart raced as I didn't know how much I depended on his physical closeness to keep me calm. He was the only one so far who was nice to me or even acknowledged me at all.

"What a great family reunion! Not all of you made even the funeral itself." You could see some start shuffling their feet or looking away at this comment. "I wanted to address the elephant in the room. This lady next to me. Stand up, Anne."

What was he doing? I could feel sweat starting to flow down my face. As I stood I hoped they couldn't see my body shaking.

"This lady here is Anne. She was asked to come because she was named as a beneficiary on our dear brother's will. Oh, and it looks like we are about to go in."

Thank goodness. All the eyes turned at the sound of the buzzer, and we all watched as the secretary picked up her phone and nodded to the instructions she was given.

"You may all go in now. Sebastian is waiting," she said.

With that, it felt like the race was on. Everyone immediately stood up, and before I knew it, I was at the back of the line heading into the room. As I walked in I noticed the light wood colors of the panels and perfectly laid furniture around the room. It looked like a room you would see that overlooked mountains and rivers. One that a friend would invite you in to drink tea, discuss the latest news, and relax by a cozy fire. Not a big-shot lawyer about to read the will of some mega-million-dollar man. I was so busy looking around at all the fine details of the room I didn't notice everyone was already seated except me. Or at least standing and paying attention.

"Will you be joining us today?"

My heart skipped a beat upon hearing the voice. An image of Brian flashed through my mind again and a tingling sensation ran up my spine. I turned to find the speaker and stopped in my tracks. He looked nothing like Brian. This man made Brian look like a boy. He looked like he had been chiseled out of the smoothest, most beautiful white stone one could imagine. His dark brown hair was thick and wavy, and his eyes were the brightest blue I had ever seen. I wanted to dive right in and forget all my worries. His lips were turned up on one corner as if in amusement. Amusement? *Oh shit.* Once again all 25 pairs of eyes were looking at me. Some were hiding behind their hands trying not to laugh. My face had turned red by now and thank goodness for Jack who patted the spot next to him. I quickly sat down and made myself as small as I could.

"Now that we are all here, let's commence. We are here today for the reading of the will of Sir Anthony Wilkens. Now, usually I would have sent this out to all of you to read on your own, but we have a special situation here, and I wanted to do it in person to not have any confusion." At this, he looked over at the well-dressed pantsuit lady. "The last will and testament was last modified on Wednesday, May 5, 2010, per Sir Anthony Wilkens' request. It was signed and notarized by two witnesses: Andy Miller and Marjorie Cook. As we all know, much of your family's wealth was passed to Anthony being the oldest and the one who carried on the family business. And before anyone asks, his long-time physician was on hand to sign a letter stating to his health and sound mind when signing.

"Are there any questions so far?" again looking at the well-dressed pantsuit lady and her family. There were shakes of heads from all in the room, and you could feel the tension rising. It was getting really stuffy in here.

"I leave, to my brother Jack, the cottage and land by the sea for his retirement because I know this spot was very special to your dear Alice. I moved some of my books and art pieces to the cottage as well. Ones I know you coveted. I hope this brings you solace as you did me when I lost a loved one. Know you are deeply loved."

I looked over at Jack and saw him beam with happiness. They must have had a wonderful relationship. Not for the first time, I wished I had grown up with a sibling.

"I leave, to my sister Bernice, 200 million dollars and five percent stock in Wilkens and Sons Inc. to split as she sees fit. You are the most accomplished of the lot of us and I have always admired the way you forged your own path when there was no path made for you. You are an outstanding female role model to all our nieces. Your sons make me proud, and I'm proud to have lived long enough to see your grandkids and great-grandkids. I also leave you the tools from our shed. Any that the household no longer needs and that you can see fit to use. Your favorite horse is also groomed and ready for you to bring home. I love you very much."

Bernice was crying in her husband's arms and saying thank you over and over again. Her husband had tears in his eyes as well.

"I leave to my sister Catherine 250 million dollars and five percent stock in Wilkens and Sons Inc. to split as she sees fit. You have always made me laugh and could always get me out of one of my moods with one of your crazy outfits and by just being you. Your brood of kids are wonderful, and I am glad to see that laughter was a trait that was passed down through your family. I also leave you the closet full of clothes from Mom. I think Lauren could use them well in her theater work. I love you dearly."

"I leave to my sister Geraldine 100 million dollars to split as she sees fit. Please know that I wish I could have been there for you more when you were growing up. I feel to a certain extent that your love for physical objects, your constant need for attention, and your lack of common etiquette toward your fellow humans comes from a lack of love when you were younger. There was so much turmoil right before your teenage years, and I apologize for the heartache that might have caused you. I wish you no ill will, but I have to look out for the family business."

There were audible gasps from the group and a chuckle from Jack next to me. If I didn't know any better, he was having a grand time with this whole event. Others started crying, some started to shout about the unfair treatment of their parents with how the money was divided. There was chaos starting to ensue, and all I could do was sit there glued to my seat. Who had ever heard of so much money? Why in the world was I here?

Then Sebastian looked at me with amused eyes and said "Please, everyone quiet down. We are not done yet. There is one more person." Once again, every eye turned to me, and I could hear Jack trying to hold back a laugh. I was definitely red in the face.

"Anthony wrote a letter, and he would like me to read it aloud to all of you."

My Dear Lovely Family,

If you are hearing this, then I have passed on and Sebastian is reading you my will. You will have noticed that there is a young Chinese girl in the audience and that is not by accident. My siblings might have a clue as to who she is, but for the rest of you, it is up to your parents to divulge the family secret if they want to. I know some wish it to be buried as they think it brought shame to our family. However, our family has survived, the company is doing well, and I see no reason to hide it anymore. I have lived this long life in a lie and owe my wife, Sally, much in forgiveness and to many in my past. I can only hope that this small act will right some wrongs and bring some good karma back into this family.

Anne, please do with these gifts as you wish. But do know that if I had known earlier, I would have loved you like a granddaughter.

Love, your adoring older brother,
Anthony

.   .   .

Jack was laughing so hard he almost fell out of his chair. What was up with people and laughing when it came to this will and me? The others were either stone-faced, curious, or outright glaring at me. The room became so silent.

"I leave to Anne Huang, daughter of Josephine Lin, grand-daughter of Rose Chen, Seaside Mansion, the rest of my monetary fortune, my two properties overseas, and anything else that was missed in this will."

"How much was the rest of his fortune?"

"Jacqueline, we do not ask out right in front of strangers, especially strangers not in the family," Geraldine said while glaring at me. "I'm sure Sebastian will divulge that when we can talk in private." She gave Sebastian a knowing look.

"Actually, Anthony told me that if needed I should share the amount with all of you while you're here."

"Oh, this is going to be good," said Jack under his breath.

"Are you sure he was in a sound mind when he signed this?" said Jacqueline.

"Here's the doctor's note if you care to read it."

"No, no. But I would like to know the amount."

"Jacqueline, we all know your uncle Anthony did very well, and it's probably an exorbitant amount of money. It's not like the rest of us were worse off. He took care of us when Dad didn't. The rest of us would like to go home," said Bernice who had started looking at her watch.

"Of course you all would. You got more money from uncle Anthony. Cleary, he spited us and I would like to know just how much this stranger is running off with," making a point of staring at me.

"Fine. Go ahead, Sebastian. Please entertain us with how rich my brother was."

"Anne will be receiving Seaside Mansion worth roughly 100 million. There are two other properties that are worth about 35 million together. After probate, distributing the money allocated to you guys, adding in the stock options for the business, he will have about two billion left in cash. That doesn't take into account the artwork and other collectibles he has acquired through his life. I believe that is all. If there are no further questions, I will be contacting you in the next couple weeks about your distributions."

There was a deafening silence in the room. Apparently, no one had any idea he had amassed that much wealth. I was in complete shock, frozen in my seat, and I didn't even know if I was breathing anymore. A chair moved, and when I looked up, I saw Geraldine's family looking at me before they stormed off. The looks on Geraldine and Jacqueline's faces would have melted me right where I was sitting if not for Jacqueline's other siblings who gave me looks of pity as they followed their mother out the door.

Jacqueline went and whispered something in Sebastian's ear. He nodded in response. A stab of jealousy came out of nowhere seeing her get so close to him before I realized I must be crazy. Somehow, I shook hands with Bernice and Catherine before their families left as well. They were polite but also in shock. They wished me well and left just as quickly. I was left with Jack and Sebastian who were talking gaily as if what just happened was an everyday occurrence. Then a thought came to me; maybe in their world, it was.

Jack walked over and gave me a kiss on my hand. "Welcome to the family."

"How—How come he didn't give you any money?"

"That's your first question?" he looked bemused, but what he didn't know was I felt like I was floating, watching the whole scene from above. I didn't even know what I was saying or asking anymore. "He knew I didn't need any. It was no secret that I was my father's favorite. When he passed away, I was very well taken care of. I never had children, and I've invested well, so there was no need for me to take more. He always got along with his nieces and nephews, and he knew his youngest sister would never let it go if he didn't give her something. Unfortunately, she raised her kids the same way she was raised. But most of them are lovely people, so I wouldn't worry. They're all harmless. All bark and no bite."

"That's very thoughtful of you," I looked at him—a little disbelieving.

"Someone in the family had to be," he winked. "I told you, don't let them get to you. Sebastian has my number if you ever need help. I have to run otherwise I would have loved to chat with you more, but it was nice to meet you. Sebastian, good to see you again." As Sebastian shook his hand, I saw Jack lean closer and whisper something to Sebastian. I saw a quick glimpse in my direction, and in a blink, I was alone in the office with Sebastian. He walked over with a big smile on his face which I wanted to wipe right off.

"Well, welcome to the family. You've created quite a stir. I wouldn't worry about them too much. Sir Anthony was adamant about the change, and we made it clear the houses and money were to go to you." He seemed so nonchalant about the whole thing I started getting irritated.

"I didn't even know the guy and why not include my mother in the will, too? How did he know my family? Why would he give us so much? Why would he give us anything at all? And you mentioned a change. Did he add me last minute? Why?" I almost screamed. I gasped for breath and sank back in my chair.

"Calm down," he said, laughing. "These are all good things happening. I don't know the answers to your questions, but I have an envelope to give you that can get you started."

Sebastian went to his desk and unlocked one of his drawers. He took out what looked like a simple white envelope. I noticed his fingers were long and soft. A jolt went through me when his hand brushed against mine, and I quickly stuffed my hand and the envelope into my purse so he wouldn't see me shaking.

"You should find all the information you need about the house as well as bank account information. When you arrive at the house Andy will fill you in on other details and provide you with a set of keys. Anthony asked me to check in on you from time to time to see how you're doing, so I'll see you this week. Also, here is the number for your driver."

He's going to come see me? My driver? Breathe...

"The family is complicated, but he loved his family and felt like he should support all of them despite his feelings for them, but you got the bulk of his wealth and his favorite house. That house was his pride and joy."

By this time, he was standing right next to me, and I could smell his cologne, which reminded me of a cool, spring day. Good thing I caught myself before I leaned in too much.

"It's all very generous. I'm in a bit of a shock and having a hard time processing everything. I think I should go now," I said while I backed toward the door. "You had mentioned two other properties. Where are they?"

"One is on Maui in Hawaii. Beautiful place. Opens to the ocean. The whole family used to go once a year when everyone was younger. The other property is in Taipei, Taiwan. That one was private just for Sir Anthony. I would keep that property between us."

Taiwan! What is going on?

I think I gave him a blank stare, quickly thanked him, and walked out of his office. I needed to find Victoria before I went home to my mom.

5

I DROVE non-stop back to Astoria where Victoria met me at Market Cafe. Over pizza, I told her what happened at the will reading. She listened intently and for once didn't disturb me while I talked. At the end, I waited for her usual outbursts of excitement or the poking fun at me because I was enraptured by a strange man, but she just sat there and stared at me.

"Oh . . . my . . . god! I have the richest friend in the whole wide world!" She ran over and gave me the biggest of hugs. A huge weight lifted now that I knew I hadn't shocked my friend into silence, and she was exhibiting what I thought I should be feeling. "We will celebrate. And you can't say no. You're not traveling, you have no itinerary at the moment, and you're loaded so you can afford anything you want!"

"Not so loud," I hissed.

"Come on, dance with me."

"Victoria!" I tried not to laugh. "I need you to talk some sense into me before I go home to tell my mom. My head is spinning."

"Anne, you deserve all of this. Just accept it. You have so much money now you can literally do whatever you want. You can take care of your mom. You two can go on that Taiwan trip you keep talking about. You'll have a house big enough, you could have her move in if you wanted. Or you could even have her live in the house, and you could go live in one of your other houses—or even buy brand-new houses for the both of you. You could travel the world forever. Plus, you can go buy a new wardrobe. Impress that boy you're infatuated with."

"What boy?" I asked trying to hide the blush coming to my face.

"What boy? I know you too well for you to pull that on me. Like I was saying, we will go shopping for a whole new wardrobe. You are my oldest friend. Most people ditch me after a few years. Somehow you've hung around and let me tag along on your adventures. Just go home, tell your mom, sleep on it. Just let it soak in and stop trying to process it. It's not lab data that you can analyze to the dot."

"You sound way too reasonable right now."

"That's me. The voice of reason," she said with a big smile.

"Yeah, right," I laughed.

I arrived home after dinner and saw my mom watching her Korean soap opera. Both eyes were closed, but I didn't dare walk over to turn off the TV. I wasn't ready to talk to her yet. A wave of nostalgia swept through me as I looked around my bedroom. Just me and my mom since I could remember. My hand brushed the envelope in my purse, and I took it out and flipped it around in my hand. I was rich. Stupid rich. A slow grin spread across my lips as I fell asleep.

6

I woke up blurry-eyed and stared out the window cursing the sun for rising once again. Sleep had evaded me as I tossed and turned all night. As soon as I drifted off, Sebastian showed up. I couldn't get rid of him. He would show up at the mansion. He was showing me around, holding my hand, looking back at me with those magnificent blue eyes that wrapped me up in warmth. I would switch to a grocery store, the most boring place to meet someone, he would be the cashier and I would watch those long fingers grabbing each item. I would go to the middle of the desert and he would emerge from behind every rock or cactus.

"Anne, get up! Why did you not wake me up last night to tell me what happened? You left me on the couch sleeping!"

I popped one eye open and saw my mom hovering over me with her hands on her waist and the aroma of breakfast wafting in the air. Without fail, she always had warm food ready in the morning.

"I'm up. I'll tell you over breakfast," I mumbled.

"No breakfast for you until you tell me what happened at the reading yesterday."

"Okay, okay, I'm getting up."

I rolled out of bed, still in the clothes from yesterday, while Mom huffed out of my room. Slowness was the key this morning, but I couldn't take *too* long, so after the basic grooming I moseyed into the kitchen and sat down in front of my food.

Mom was waiting with rapt attention—not even touching her food yet.

"The reading was something else. I met his brother, sisters, and his niece and nephews. His brother is very nice and received a cottage to retire in. The sisters each received 100–250 million dollars to be divided up as they wished, and we received everything else."

"And that would be?"

"We got his house, his property in Maui, and his property in Taiwan so we can finally go there now!"

"Not now Anne. Anything else?"

"And close to two billion dollars in cash." Mom was staring at me with her mouth open and her eyes bulging wide. She suddenly stood up, walked out of the kitchen and into her room, and . . . silence. I sat there unsure how to react as usually she's telling me what to do or talking non-stop to express everything she's feeling. Rustling emanated from her room and I went to look.

"Mom, are you okay?"

"I'm fine. I'm just tidying up."

I watched as she moved picture frames on her bedside table. Dusted shelves that had probably been dusted yesterday. Shuffled her clothes around in her closet. Swatted at the drapes. Then she collapsed into her chair and started sobbing. I ran to her and put my arms around her. This was not what I expected.

"We don't have to accept it. I know you have provided a very good life for us and I love our home here. His niece seemed very upset about losing the house so I'm sure they would be more than happy to get it."

She looked at me with renewed strength.

"Silly girl. Why would we give back what was legally given to us? We don't have to worry where the money is going to come from anymore. Why would we give that up?"

"But we don't even know this man."

"Clearly, there is some connection and a big one at that for him to give you the majority of his wealth. It behooves you to at least find out why. Was I mentioned in the will?

"No."

"Figures. Your Ai Po was the first in this country, but she rarely talked about her past. She always said the past was best left in the dust and we should only look toward the future as the future is where the light is. I never liked that. I only know she came from Taiwan."

"Why do you say figures?"

"Oh, nothing. I'm old and he probably wanted to give it to someone young who would last for a while. I wouldn't be surprised if you're expected to run his company, too."

"Um, run a company?"

"Don't worry about it. Just breathe, Anne. One step at a time," Mom said as she came over and held me. "I know all of this is a lot. We'll take it in stride."

"Well, I have the address to the house so we could go visit if you would like. Maybe there's buried treasure," I said trying to lighten the mood.

"Yes, let's go. Adventures have always done us well. I bet it's covered in dust and we'll have to spend millions getting it cleaned and restored."

"Way to be positive, Mom. Let me check." I went to look through the envelope. "It's in the hills of Portland." I flipped the paper over and realized I had forgotten about the phone number. "Sebastian gave me a phone number. He said it was for our driver," I noticed a slight quiver in my voice when I said his name.

"Our driver?" my mom's eyes had gotten enormous again.

"That's what he said. I'll give him a call and see if he can pick us up. Worse case we drive there ourselves."

"And what did you think of Sebastian?"

"What do you mean? He's the lawyer. The one that read the will yesterday. He's supposed to be stopping by this week to make sure we transition well. You'll get to meet him."

"Okay," giving me a long look. Maybe she had heard the quiver in my voice as well. I can only hope not.

7

WE LEFT the city and went down roads that were void of buildings as far as the eye could see. The driver hadn't hesitated when I called. He showed up in a full black suit driving a Rolls Royce. Mom and I stared at him for I don't know how long. He was too polite to say a word, but I thought I saw signs of a smirk.

Two hours later we came in on a driveway that seemed never-ending and was lined with trees groomed to perfection. Between the rich creamy leather of the seats, the scent of oranges that filled the car, and the serenity the view provided it was magical and did not feel like someone's home. The pathway ended in a circular driveway with a big fountain in the middle. Inside the fountain was a lady looking back at a little boy. Their faces were carved with happy lines, and they looked like they were chasing each other through the fountain and enjoying life to the fullest. The lady looked like she had narrow eyes, a flatter nose . . . and then there was the house. I glued my face to the window. It easily spread across a whole block with miles of greenery as far as the eye could see. The beauty of this place was set in its simple, clean design, but the expanse of it was mind-boggling. How did one person own all of this?

The door was three times my size. It could be a giant

masquerading as a door and I wouldn't know it. I'd just be looking at one leg! I quickly put my hands in my pockets to keep them from shaking. What was I thinking that I had a right to this house just because some piece of paper said so? Mom couldn't even talk reason into me. She came along! While I was waiting, my mind started racing to all sorts of embarrassing scenarios mainly not being posh enough for a grand place like this. The image of a mansion-owner was not what I would think of as *me*. I was a lowly servant compared to people who lived in this society. Smart, successful, lowly servant— but lowly servant just the same. His sister's family was proof of that. Why was no one answering? I was starting to shake even with all my layers. Looking back the way we came I wondered if it was too late to run.

The door suddenly opened while I was lost in thought, and I was starting to get numb. I looked up and saw an older gentleman in a black suit with white gloves looking at me with a passive but kind face. His head was starting to bald with wisps of white hair on the sides. He must be the Andy that Sebastian had mentioned.

"May I help you?"

"Yes," I stammered. "My name is Anne, and this is my mom. We just learned we had . . ."

"Oh yes, Sebastian told me you two might be stopping by soon. Please come in. Boots under the seat, and I will take your jackets."

I rushed in without hesitating and left a streak of snow behind me. No time to feel guilty about spotting the perfectly polished floor. The warmth of the house enveloped me. A house I didn't even know existed yesterday. This was just too surreal. I put my boots under the bench and stayed there for a bit while the heat from the floorboards blew up into my face. The warmth made me feel more comfortable, and I started to relax a bit. I handed my coat to Andy and looked around for the first time. The entrance was one to rival Scarlett's when she made her appearance at the top of the stairs. The grand staircase went up to the second floor and split in two directions lining the second floor with an impressive hallway filled with what looked like paintings and family photos. Chandeliers hung at every corner with the biggest hanging right over me lighting the foyer in a bright white light showing every detail of the architecture. Carvings were done in every wood piece lining the stairway, the columns in the hallway, the door I just walked through, and more. I could have stood there for hours just exploring the artistic details of the foyer. All the walls were painted a warm, cream color that made the wood carvings stand out and become works of art in their own right.

A tantalizing aroma was wafting in from a room in front of me, but before I could ask I was ushered into the room on my right. Through double doors, I saw a fireplace that was burning bright and warm. I instantly gravitated to it, crossing a couple high-back armchairs and two large sofas. Mom and I sat down on one of the sofas. It felt good to be warm again. Andy settled himself on the other sofa. That's when I looked up. On all four walls were books from floor to ceiling. The only places there weren't books were the double doors I just came in from and two large windows with window seating that looked back out at the front lawn. Thick, carpet-like curtains draped the windows, making them look like elegantly dressed ladies dancing by the fireside. Sunlight came in showing off the reading nooks in the walls, beautiful carvings that matched the rest of the house, a large wooden table with its own high-back chair off on one side, and the light dust hovering in the air that seemed to be a permanent part of any library. The books called out to me and I hoped to spend a lot of time in this room.

"Please, make yourself comfortable. Some tea and snacks will be brought up soon. I decided for us to meet in this room for today as it stays the warmest during winter. Lord Anthony Wilkens, Sir Anthony Wilkens' father, was an avid reader and liked his human comforts. Ah, here are tea and snacks now."

A cart rolled in pushed by a girl not more than fifteen. She was wearing a white dress with a black apron around her waist. She pushed the cart right between us and set everything on the table.

"Is there anything else you need?" she seemed shy and looked like she was trying to look everyone in the eyes but failing miserably.

"No, this is more than generous, and what is your name?" I asked to try to make her more comfortable.

"Lavender, Ma'am. I've been here since I was ten. Came with my mom when she started working here and they let me do small things here and there."

"Lavender, thank you for bringing up the tea and snacks. I'm sure Cook is looking for you," said Andy.

"Oh, Cook said for you all to come down to the kitchen when you're done up here as she'd like to meet the new owner and get a feel for where she stands."

At this, Andy's eyebrows seemed to tighten, and a frown came across his face, but he kept his countenance, which wasn't exactly what my mom and I were doing. Owner. This was a foreign word to me and I wasn't sure I liked it.

"Lavender, tell Cook we will head down *if* we finish up here, and that we will have a discussion later," Andy said with some sternness.

Lavender realized she had said too much, nodded a quick affirmation of having heard, and quickly walked back out of the library.

"I am sorry for her comment, but since she has mentioned it, I should warn you. The staff here are worried you will fire them, and they are unhappy for the moment. I assured them that you would not be doing such a thing. You do not seem like an unreasonable person, but on the other hand, none of us know each other well yet. And on that note, I wanted to ask you if the staff could have a week off? It's been six months, but many are scared they'll lose their job if they leave town."

"Of course!"

"That's great to hear. I will let them know. By the way, please call me Andy. I came to work in this house as a little boy when Lord Anthony Wilkens was still head of the household."

"Wow, you've been here a long time. I thought butlers and servants were only in books and movies. I think I can say that I will not be making any drastic decisions any time soon. This was such a surprise, and I am still in shock for what I have received." Especially my mom who looked like she was going to hyperventilate at any moment. She hadn't said a word since we got into the car.

"I'm sure you both would love to see the house? Would you like a tour once you've warmed up a bit more?"

"That would be lovely. I'm so impressed by the details in the wood and how everything works together to give off such an elegance."

"In the meantime, we can go over some logistics." Andy pulled a set of keys and handed them to me. Each key was labeled: main house, garage, cottage, pool, etc.

"Here is your set of keys to the entire property. We'll do a little of the tour each day so as not to overwhelm you, but do let me know if you have any places you really want to visit. You are free to roam when you please, of course. You are the new master of this house. I hope you grow to love this place as much as Sir Anthony and the rest of the staff. The staff live in the rooms on the bottom floor, below the one we're on now. Your rooms would be upstairs, and they are prepared for both of you to move in as soon as you would like."

"Oh, I don't think we'll be moving in. I'm not sure what we would do with a place this big. Plus, I move around a lot. I travel for work and my mom has her studio back in Portland set up exactly the way she likes it. I did bring stuff to stay a couple nights just to see the place."

"There's no need to make rash decisions. Your room will be ready when and if you would like to move in. Do you have any questions so far?" asked Andy.

"No, but Mom, you haven't said one word. Is there anything you would like to ask?" Her face was getting more and more lines on it the longer we were here. I was getting worried she might be coming down with something. She looked so pale and worn out.

"No, actually I would like to go home. Anne, please stay. Find out more, but I need to go home now. I'm not feeling well," Mom stood up abruptly almost knocking her tea off the table.

"Mom, I'll come home with you. You're not yourself and I'm worried."

"I am a grown woman and I can get home just fine. I will ask the driver to come straight back to get you so you don't have to wait too long if you want to head home later. I just need to rest and settle myself."

"Are you sure?"

"Stay. What do you think I do with myself every day? You think I sit around in front of the TV and never venture out on my own? That I have no friends or events to go to? I would have you know that I go and converse with Abigail next door every morning, and we chit chat about you kids. I have lunch every once in a while with Amy, too. I frequent the public library and I keep myself busy without your help."

"Mom, I wasn't trying to offend you." I backed up and let my mom stomp out of the library. I followed after and watched as she dressed for the cold. The driver was already at the entrance and I watched as they drove off down the long pathway.

I couldn't figure out what had gotten into her. The massiveness of the place suddenly made me feel very lonely where I didn't know a soul, not even the previous owner. Her presence here meant more to me than I had thought. She was a warmth of familiarity that I needed. Now it was just me. At least the house wasn't completely empty of human life. I shuddered at the thought of exploring this place on my own.

Walking back to the library I saw Andy was waiting on the couch. He didn't say a word as I took a sip of tea letting the warmth flow down me and allowing the fire to warm me again. I looked up at Andy and said, "Do you know why I've inherited the house?"

"That's not for me to say."

"So you do. Why can't you say?"

"All in good time. Would you like to start with the tour?"

"Okay, I'll let it go for now. I'm ready for the tour. Let's do this."

Andy immediately stood up, "I believe you will really learn to love this house." He had been completely deadpan this whole time, and I was starting to wonder if he ever smiled or showed any emotions.

𝕾 8 𝕾

WE STARTED in the library since we were already there. Lord Anthony, Sir Anthony's father, knew he would frequent this room the most and hence he put it at the front of the house. This gave him easy access to the entrance with a view of the front lawn, so he could see the comings and goings of anyone exiting or entering the house. He was a stickler for knowing everything that happened in the household, so the house was run on a very precise time schedule. Suffice it to say the turnaround of workers here was high, and he did not make a lot of friends with the staff. The long table had been his desk and the sofas his lounge as well as for guest entertainment, which he enjoyed immensely. Sir Anthony took after his father with his love of books and also used the library as his office.

"But Sir Anthony, you will learn, was very different from his father in many ways. We all loved him dearly and are extremely sad that he has passed. Not much has changed as to the layout, decoration, or furniture. These are all originals. The books have been collected by the family for many generations and some are one of a kind and very precious. We get scholars in here from time to time because we have the only resource for their topic of interest. I understand you used to be an engineer and now travel a lot. Maybe you also will find something here that will help in your endeavors. Do you like books, Anne?"

"Do I? If I could collect every book in the world I would and this room is just astounding. I can't even fathom owning all of this much less the house. I'm hoping to spend more time in this room. And if I can find books that bring me on new adventures around the world then that's an added bonus."

Andy seemed to relax a little around me. I was glad to see him relax. It was very odd to have others looking to me for approval.

My stomach grumbled and Andy must have heard it because he said, "Let's go meet Cook. Lovely woman, but she's the real person who runs this household."

We walked out of the library toward the direction of the tantalizing smell. My stomach rumbled in anticipation, and I realized that I had been here a lot longer than I thought. Several hours had passed since breakfast. Through the door was a back hallway. We commenced down the stairs in front of us and entered into a large kitchen. The kitchen was so immense I didn't know where to look first.

There were people everywhere. Some were chopping, some were washing, some were running from one room to another, but not a single person was still. Doorways led to other rooms, and I wondered where they went. A lady in a white chef's outfit seemed to be running the show. She had bright, red, frizzy hair and carried herself through the kitchen like a lion-tamer scrutinizing everyone's next move. But the one who came over to us looked like a clone, only older. She was about five feet tall and easily 150 pounds. She looked as old as Andy and not someone I wanted to mess with.

"Ah! You must be Anne. We have been awaiting your arrival. Before I give you a tour, my name is Marjorie. My mom thought it was the feminine version of margarine, and she loved working in the kitchen. Hence, my love of the kitchen. Everyone calls me Cook, so I rarely respond to Marjorie, but I do miss my name at times so feel free to use it. This is my daughter, Jasmine. She will be the next head cook here." She said that like it was a fact she was daring me to contradict.

"Thanks for letting me know," I said, liking her already.

"Sir Anthony used to love coming down here to see us cook, and he tasted every new recipe I ever made. Let me show you around. You can help yourself to anything here when you are hungry. I have just made my latest version of carrot cake. Come, come, I just put fresh icing on. You must tell me how it is."

Andy and I did not hesitate. We followed her around the kitchen and ended at a large table where the carrot cake sat front and center waiting for us to cut into it. Cook commenced to slice two big helpings and placed them on round, white plates which she served to us with dainty dessert forks. I never understood the use of dainty forks. At home, we used chopsticks for everything except for the rare occasions a chopstick didn't work—we had one fork for those instances. But I accepted it gleefully and took my first bite. The richness and sweetness exploded in my mouth and every taste worked together perfectly. I had never tasted a carrot cake this good before.

We sat there and enjoyed our cakes under the eyes of Cook. I looked up after I finished and found quizzical eyes staring back at me, probing me for my thoughts.

"Well, what do you think?"

"That was the most delicious carrot cake I have ever eaten. How did you get it to taste so moist and flavorful?"

"I changed up some spices and pulled some tricks that I learned from my own mother," she said, and I knew I wasn't going to get anything out of her. She wasn't going to tell me her secret, but I hoped I would be able to eat more of her cooking down the road.

"How long have you been here?"

"I have been here since before you were even thought of. I came about the same time as Andy. Long enough to know how to run this kitchen and keep everyone fed and happy."

"If your cooking is as good as this carrot cake . . ."

"It's better! I will cook you dinner tonight. You and your mother must stay tonight and eat. By the way, where is your mother?"

"She wasn't feeling well and had to go home. I am quite worried about her. Could I take a raincheck for dinner? I very much look forward to it, but I must get home to check on my mom."

"Of course! Here, take some of this light soup I just made and bring it home for both you and your mom to have for dinner. You will learn that a wholesome meal is always ready for breakfast, lunch, and dinner here. I do not want to see you eating snacks during meal time. Do you understand?"

"Yes, yes I do," I said, a bit startled, and also liking the fact that she was looking after me.

While I walked back toward the stairs, Andy held back to talk with Cook. They didn't hide the occasional look at me and that they were talking about me, but I liked Marjorie. She was like the Ai Po I never had. My thoughts wondered to what Andy had said about the servants being worried I would not take care of them. I hoped I was strong enough to show that I was not cruel and would try my best to keep everyone's jobs in mind. It made me nervous to have other people's fates in my hands and made me a little resentful that this was thrown on me—probably as a kind gesture, but most likely with no idea how much of a burden it would be. It was one thing to be in charge of my own life, but to have other people's lives I had to decide on—it wasn't fair.

I walked back up to the foyer and waited for Andy taking the time to look at more of the carvings in the walls. It looked like every cut was part of a grander design, and it was all over the foyer and just stunning. The light seemed to have been set to reflect from the designs to show them off.

"I expect this has been quite a morning for you and you need some space to let everything soak in," said Andy as he came out the door.

"It's been wonderful, but yes, overwhelming. Everyone has been so kind, but I should go home to check on my mom."

"Yes, yes, take your time. There is no deadline, and this is your home now. You can leave the stuff you brought here if you want. No need to bring stuff back and forth."

"Thank you, Andy. That's a great idea."

I looked out at the great expanse of the property as I walked back out the front door. The crisp air woke me up and cleared my brain. I wondered why mom had run off like that? Why Andy wasn't surprised by her leaving so suddenly? My home. Would I ever think of this as my home?

9

I DIDN'T EVEN NOTICE the scenery on the way home. All I noticed was my door opening and me walking up the stairs. Mom was nowhere to be seen. A note on the kitchen counter said, "Do not worry, I am out grocery shopping. I needed to do something productive. There is some leftover food from this morning in the refrigerator."

Thank goodness she wasn't home. For once, I really liked the idea of having my own place to go home to, where I could call my own. Some privacy especially after traveling. Hunger was never a problem here, and it seemed I would never go hungry at the mansion either. I grabbed some food and sat at the table looking out at my neighborhood. This was home. Every nook and cranny was imbedded in me inside and out. All our neighbors were pretty much the same as when I grew up here. We all looked out for each other as equals. There were families that came from all over the world, and I loved learning about all their cultures. It was what spurred me to keep traveling. How could I ever consider anywhere else home?

"Did you hear what Abigail said?"

I jumped out of my seat and turned around. How did I not hear my mom come in? She must have seen that she had surprised me because she started laughing. She went to the kitchen and started putting groceries away.

"How did you know I was home?"

"I know you. No matter where you go in this world you always come home. I could tell the mansion was overwhelming you so when I came home I went and bought groceries."

"I was thinking about our home and how I grew up here. It's the longest I've ever lived in a place. How can I ever call another place home?"

Mom turned to look at me.

"I took you when you were younger to travel the world so you could see new places, meet new people. I have never stopped you from continuing that and have never asked you to settle down. You were raised here and I will always have a room for you to stay in, but this is not your be all end all home. What a great opportunity this new inheritance will be for you."

"Mom, this inheritance is yours, too, as far as I'm concerned. You can move out with me if you're so adamant about me moving. We can both start anew . . ."

"No, I am old. As I said, this is my home. I have made my life and I like it just fine. All this new inheritance is too much for me. I do not want anything to do with it."

I suddenly remembered what my mom had said when she came home. "What did Abigail say?"

"Abigail already knows we inherited the house. It's the talk amongst the girls. I am mortified as now everyone is looking at me as if I'm the rich lady that will need to show off her wares. Money brings trouble. It always does."

"Mom, I can still sell it or give it back to the family."

"I complain, but I no longer have to worry about you making ends meet. You can go do whatever your heart desires. I will use some of the funds to keep paying for this place and make sure I have a comfortable life. Does that suit you?"

"Well, yes, it does, but are you sure?"

"Yes, yes, I'm sure. Have I ever been wishy-washy on my decisions?"

That she definitely had not. We agreed to this plan and left it at that. I would move over this weekend and visit Mom when I wanted and vice versa.

❧ 10 ❧

I CALLED the house saying that I would be moving in over the weekend and to inform everyone there that I would not be visiting before then. Work became my main focus for the rest of the week catching up on articles I had to submit to journals about my last trip to California. Our trips had brought us to Yosemite three times, San Francisco, Los Angeles, and a road trip up the entire Route 1. We stopped to swim in the ocean, dug our feet in the sand, visited the seal cave and Hearst Castle, and saw many other attractions. The work included sorting through all of my photos, touching them up, and writing a blog for each city or location. I loved doing this, but my mind just couldn't wrap itself around work today.

I was an overnight billionaire! I could do whatever I wanted now! That thought alone made me excited and scared at the same time. There was this freedom to travel without worry anymore, but what if I overdid it and I went through the money so fast I couldn't regenerate it fast enough? I had no concept what a billion dollars entailed. Since I couldn't concentrate on my blog or any of the articles I had promised to journals, I Googled "what is possible with a billion dollars?" Of course resorts, vacation homes, remote travel destinations popped up, but what caught my eye was the title "Unknown Anne Huang New Heiress to Wilkens Fortune" and the description below was "An unknown girl from the town of Astoria has inherited the majority of the Wilkens Fortune. Sir Anthony Wilkens passed away earlier this year, and it was a shock to all members of the family when this Chinese-American girl of no relations and of no lineage came on the scene." *What?!!*

It hadn't even crossed my mind that I would be in the news. I had remembered Sebastian saying something about keeping everything hush-hush until all the distributions were finalized, but here in broad daylight was a whole article about me inheriting the house, the other properties, the fact that the family never knew there was a third property, speculation on who I was—and what stung was the focus on the fact that I was Chinese-American.

The last two days went by fast and the weekend was upon me before I knew it. Most of my items were packed leaving only the necessary items at home for when I stayed over. The driver picked me up around 9:30 a.m. and I cried most of the way there. I felt like I had left myself back in Astoria with Mom. This was the first time I had actually moved away. I didn't count my stays in dormitories while in college because I always came home for holidays and summer break. My travels were always temporary, and I always came back to my mom's place at some point to unload and repack. It felt weird to have a place of my own now. My daydreams had always been a one-room studio with one wall covered in bricks. Beautiful throws from different countries would divide up the rooms for privacy, including a kitchen to cook aromatic food and a dining room to entertain my friends from abroad. The dreams never included moving into a mansion with land as far as the eye could see and to have my own staff. That in itself made me very uncomfortable. I was always self-sufficient and having staff seemed quite the opposite.

We showed up at the house right before lunch and Andy was at the door waiting for me. The heat in the house was so nice. I didn't shiver at all as I did back home. My first thought was that it must cost a fortune to heat this whole place. The fire in the library was already roaring, and I took some tea while enjoying the view of books and warmth. My stomach was rumbling, and I remembered Cook said food would always be ready. I went out to the entrance to look for Andy and to find out where I could move all my bags to. Andy was standing in an empty foyer.

"Your bags have already been moved to your room."

"Oh, that was really nice of you," I said, not sure if I should follow him to my room or get the food I really wanted.

"How is your mother doing? We were surprised by your sudden decision to move here permanently," said Andy, saving me from my awkwardness.

"She's doing well. She has an art show in a couple of weeks, so she's back to her routine of painting and gossiping, and she's comfortable at home. I don't know about permanent, but we decided that it would be good for me to have a change in my life and why not stay here while I learn everything I need to?"

"Ah, I understand. We are all very happy to have you here no matter how long you stay."

At that point, my stomach grumbled so loud Andy took notice and mentioned Cook had made a special lunch that he thought I would enjoy.

I started toward the stairs to go down into the kitchen but heard a small cough behind me. Andy gestured to my left, and I realized, of course, there was a dining area and I wasn't expected to eat in the kitchen. We went down a corridor that led away from the library and ended up in a sitting room overlooking the back of the house. There was a table set for two but could easily fit three more. The wall facing outside was floor-to-ceiling glass allowing you to almost have a 3D view of your surroundings. The amazing thing was when Andy went and opened up one of the glass walls. What I thought was a window was actually two big doors that folded sideways, and all of a sudden my room extended out into the trees. I loved it and went to stand by the table in awe that I owned this place.

"Sir Anthony had this built only ten years ago. He was getting very weak and couldn't venture out for walks like he used to. Opening a window wasn't enough for him so this room allowed him to be part of the outdoors without going out."

"It's lovely. I think it's the best room here," I said, standing there awestruck at my surroundings. I could imagine Anthony and his group of friends lounging here enjoying the sunlight while drinking tea and munching on Cook's latest delicacies. I didn't want to leave.

"Your food will be here soon. Enjoy," Andy said as he started to leave the room.

"Andy, why don't you join me today? There's an extra setting here."

"I cannot join you today," said Andy right when I noticed some movement at the entrance of the room.

"I called to tell Andy this morning that I wanted to stop by to see how you were doing. I heard you moved into the house today. Welcome home," said Sebastian as he sauntered into the room looking quite dapper in his unbuttoned suit with a nicely pressed vest and a white button-down shirt. He was clean shaven and my heart sped up at the sight of him.

"I hope I'm not intruding," he said with his hands in his pockets and staring right at me.

"No, there's no intrusion. It's great to have some company here. Please join me for lunch. I've heard Cook has something special for me today."

"She always makes the best meals. I do miss them." He paced around the room not looking at me and suddenly seeming nervous. His hands kept going in and out of his pocket, and he seemed distracted. I was curious about why he was acting this way, but then Lavender came in with a cart filled with a mouth-watering aroma. We both headed to the table and my hands were shaking the food smelled so good. Sebastian loosened his tie, and I looked away before I blushed more. How was I going to be able to sit at the same table with him and only him through the whole of lunch?

When the covers were taken off the plate all I could do was stare. A huge laugh came out of Sebastian and I looked up to see the biggest smile on him. He was laughing all the way up to his eyes. The sight of fried rice on my dish and the no-restraint-laughter from Sebastian broke the tension and I started laughing as well. I had been expecting a European sit-down, fancy meal such as duck confit, but this was fried rice and it looked exactly like what my mom made at home. Fried rice was like serving mac and cheese at one of my western friend's homes.

"Cook clearly wanted to impress you today by making fried rice."

"Clearly."

"Don't look so offended. Try it. I'm sure it'll surprise you."

"You sound as if you know what you're talking about," trying to make heads or tails of the food in front of me.

"Yes, I do. Anthony asked for my guidance more and more during the last five years of his life, and I would come up to consult about any changes to his will or estate. Cook was always generous in her offerings and I had many pleasant meals here. Sometimes she would even let me sample one of her new creations. Just try the dish." He brought a spoonful of rice, meat, and carrots up to his mouth.

I dug into the fried rice and took a bite more out of politeness than actual interest and was startled. It looked the same but tasted so different and was amazing. The best fried rice I had ever had. It had the same ingredients as my mom's; rice, eggs, carrots, marinated meat, and green onions, but it was not over seasoned, just the right combination of rice, meat, and vegetables, and there was a taste to it that I couldn't quite pinpoint. I quickly ate the whole dish. Cook had really displayed her ability. Made something so simple and mundane into something quite new and enjoyable.

While Sebastian and I finished off our meals, we talked about what had happened since he last saw me in his office. He was polite and never interrupted me, agreeing with me at the right times. I learned that he was not from around here, but he did not elaborate more on his past. He had gone to school at The University of Texas at Austin and had started out interning in a local office as a clerk. He worked himself up to where he is now—mostly thanks to the Wilkens family. I got the feeling Sir Anthony's relationship with Sebastian was more than just a lawyer and client. That Sir Anthony had a big influence on his life and made him who he was today.

It was nice to talk to someone new. I usually talked to Victoria, but she was prepping for her Europe trip, so I wasn't able to see her before I left Astoria. Friendship only came easily when I was abroad. It wasn't that I didn't want friends. I looked at people in pubs hanging out with their chums, drinking a beer, and laughing at a joke someone made. I definitely wanted that, but it had always eluded me. Something about coming back to the US, I became a hermit. Maybe it was the familiarity of the place or the fact that I didn't really fit in growing up and home was my sanctuary. No one was allowed in unless they passed twenty tiers of tests. Abroad, I could open up and be who I was. There was nobody there who had known me since I was in elementary school and had embarrassing stories to tell. Maybe Mom was right, and I was still running from Brian. Talking to Sebastian was more than I had done in a long time and it was nice to meet someone new.

Sebastian suddenly stood up after we had finished eating. "I must head back to the office now. I have clients waiting. It's good to see you are settling in. I'll come back again another day and let Andy know if you need anything. He knows how to get in touch with me."

"Oh, well it was nice to see you today. Great to have lunch with you." I was a bit startled that he was leaving so abruptly. And I was just starting to enjoy his company and not feel awkward. Andy appeared out of nowhere and walked Sebastian back to the main entrance while I stayed and enjoyed the room some more. I imagined myself curling up in a window seat with a book from the library and ignoring the rest of the world. There was still no answer to why we had inherited this house and all this money, but I felt I would find out soon enough. While I was daydreaming, Andy came back with Lavender who cleared the room of any remaining evidence of lunch.

"Shall I show you to your room?"

"That would be wonderful. It would be really nice to unpack and see something familiar."

"Right this way, Miss."

❧ 11 ❧

WE WERE BACK at the entrance looking at the grand staircase. The stairs were the most prominent part of this whole entryway, and yet, I hadn't thought about them since coming in that very first time. Andy had shown me three cavernous rooms and my brain couldn't fathom that there was more to see, but one of those rooms up there was where I would lay my head down to sleep tonight. We walked up the stairs and down the right hallway. My feet started lagging because what looked like portraits from the first floor were actually detailed paintings of family patriarchs. In the background were what looked like their significant others, siblings, and children. Under each painting were their names, the years they were born, and the years they passed away. Sir Anthony's was the first painting we passed. Here was the person whom I was benefiting from, and how I wished I could have gotten to know him and thanked him in person.

Anthony had blond hair and green eyes. He had lines around his eyes that I knew too well from my mom. "Worry lines," some called them, but they framed eyes that seemed kind and gave him a youthful look.

"He was a very generous person, and everyone loved him. At least those he cared about, which were many," said Andy coming back to meet me.

We walked to the next painting that showed a man who looked very similar to Anthony, but with darker hair and steely eyes. He would be someone who I could imagine reigned over his family and exerted his power. I would not have liked to meet him.

"This is Lord Anthony Wilkens. Sir Anthony's father. He was the second Anthony in the family, which made Sir Anthony the third. He loved his family, but he had very set rules and beliefs. You would agree with him on every point if you were to be in his circle. He treated us staff members fairly, but he and Sir Anthony butted heads many times."

"How did he become head of the company and inherit all of this if he and his father butted heads so much? Jack had mentioned he was the favorite."

"Yes, Jack was the favorite, but Anthony was the oldest, and also had the most business sense much to his father's chagrin. There was no doubt in anyone's eyes that Anthony would be the one to inherit. Jack never wanted the company, so everything worked out. There is also, Lord Anthony was very traditional and always had high hopes for his son. It's one of the reasons they did not get along at times."

I understood traditions. Chinese culture was full of them. Valuing family above everything else, paying respect to your elders and never talking back no matter what, giving cash for any gift: birthdays, weddings, funerals, the birth of a child, really any occasion, and expecting your parents to live with you in their old age are just to name a few. However, I don't think it was quite the right correlation between my parents and Lord Anthony. He looked uncomfortable to be around and seemed to rule with an iron fist.

More family portraits, which I assumed were ancestors, stared back at us while we walked to my room. We occasionally stopped so I could study them, but Andy didn't provide any more information. I learned he was fourteen when he came to work for the Wilkens, and the family was very hush-hush about their past family members.

The warm, cream color and wood paneling continued on the

second floor. We walked down the hallway past four closed rooms and went up another set of stairs. These wound up like a spiral and dropped us on the third floor where skylights illuminated the hallway.

"Your room is just down the hall, a few doors down on the left," said Andy.

I immediately loved my room. The carpeted floor was so lush I dug my toes in and stood there enjoying the sensation. Sunlight shone in through three tall and slender windows starting at about four feet off the ground and reaching to a couple feet from the ceiling. Bright red, heavy drapes were pulled to either side of the windows and looked out on the front of the house. The red drapes, gold trims, and crisp air coming through the opened window made me think of Christmas coming up in a month—my favorite time of the year. The reds accented the light pink of the blossoms falling from a painted tree that arched over a door I thought was my closet—or maybe it was my bathroom. I felt like I was in a wonderland. *I could get used to this,* I thought as I took a deep breath.

I turned to see all my luggage lined up against the wall. It was surreal to see my personal items here with me. The fact I owned this house still hadn't sunk in.

"I know this has all been overwhelming, but take your time. I think you will learn to love this house as your own," said Andy.

"I think I am already starting to love this house, but I don't know how I will ever love it as my own. I have never known anything like this, much less *owned* it, especially by surprise."

"Give yourself some time. I will leave you here to unpack and settle in your room. Is there anything you need at the moment?"

"No Andy, you have been very welcoming this week, and I really appreciate it."

I laid down on the plush carpet as soon as Andy left. My whole body groaned with exhaustion from the past week, and I wondered again how Ai Po knew Sir Anthony in order for him to be so generous to me and why my mother was not included. I started following lines along the ceiling and realized I was looking at more carvings above me. A big tree trunk was painted between the windows and extended into branches that stretched to every corner of the ceiling. Between the branches were beautiful carvings with the most intricate design right over the bed. There was a ship, a house that looked like this one, horses, carriages, and blossoms everywhere. Blossoms rained down the walls, and it really felt like I was under a tree in full bloom. Whoever built this house was very much into details and I was reaping the reward of it all. I followed the twists and turns until I dozed off.

12

A FEW HOURS LATER, I woke to the sun still shining through my room and an ache down my back. For a second I wasn't sure where I was. It felt like I was sleeping on fur. Everywhere I touched was like petting a soft furry rabbit, and yet it felt like solid wood right underneath me. I focused on the ceiling, and slowly my brain started waking up and remembering my new room. My luggage was still on the side and I still had to unpack. Rolling over, I peeled myself off of the floor.

With a refreshed mind I looked at my room again with renewed eyes. It had eight sides with windows on three of them. I must be in the tower section I saw outside. A queen-size canopy-bed was on the wall to the right of the windows with a big boudoir on the other side of the room. Next to it, a door that seemed to lead to the bathroom which I made a mental note to visit soon. Hanging by the window was a painting of a Chinese girl who didn't look more than seventeen. Other images of Chinese workers standing beside half-built railroad tracks were hanging sporadically around the room. The photos of Chinese workers and the girl seemed out of place and yet fit into the room seamlessly. That made me curious if the rest of the house had pictures of Asian workers. Maybe these were people who worked for the company.

I opened up the closet to an unexpected sight—not that I was expecting anything in particular. The closet was half the size of my room, or in other words, the size of my mom's living room and kitchen combined. All of my luggage fit in a corner. There were white shelves lining all the walls and wooden rods that were polished and perfect at every angle. Some dresses were already hanging in the closet. They looked like they were from my grandparents' era. Beautiful, simple dresses. All the dresses ended below my knee and some had buttons from top to bottom along the front of the dress. All of them had cap sleeves and a different style belt custom-made to the dress. I couldn't wait to put them on! When I looked down, I noticed an old chest of dark wood. The side was chipped a bit, but overall it looked in great shape. There were carvings of mountains and trees you would see in an ancient Chinese painting. There was a pin that went through the lock in front and I wondered if I had the key to it. It was a lock I had only seen once before—on a chest in my mom's closet. The opening for the key was an H-shape with the middle section longer than the sides. I wondered if the key might be one from the keyring Andy had given me.

Remembering I had stored the keys in the library, I started to run down to get them when I saw the light blinking on my cell phone. It was Victoria! She left a message asking if it was okay for her to visit. She would take a bus to me. I was so excited I ran down to ask for the car to go pick her up. On the way down I needed to get fuel to stay focused. Plus, I didn't know where to find Andy so I'd have to look for him after.

The kitchen was just like I saw it the first time except there was no one around. I just assumed that it would always be bustling, and the emptiness threw me off a bit. But it did not deter me for long from finding the refrigerator except this was twice as big as the one at my mom's place. Most of the items on the shelves were raw goods, but I saw a container labeled 'cheesecake.' It looked like it already had a slice cut out of it so I didn't think twice before pulling it off its shelf and bringing it out to the table. If this cake was anything like the carrot cake Cook had made the first day I met her I wasn't going to pass this opportunity. I went in search of utensils and found tons of knives of varying sizes. My mom had always used a butcher knife for everything. The scale of the kitchen and supplies just baffled me. A butcher knife, chopsticks, maybe a spatula, some spoons and forks, and butter knives were pretty much all I grew up with. Cook seemed to have a gadget for anything you could dream of. I finally found my fork, cut a slice of cake onto a plate, and headed back upstairs. Being alone in an empty cavernous space was not my idea of relaxed eating.

On my way back up to the room, I passed the first door on the left after Sir Anthony's portrait. The door knob turned easily and my curiosity took over when I saw the grandiose of the room. It was twice the size of mine. Turning on the light showed a big king-size poster bed on the right far away from the door. The ceiling was painted a bright red. A color you would see in traditional Chinese ceremonies. A beautiful crystal chandelier hung in the middle of the ceiling lighting up the trim-work around the edges of the ceiling and the floor. A writing desk and high-back chair were by the window looking out at the backyard garden, which I made a mental note to visit soon. The room looked more lived-in than any of the other rooms. Piles of paper were still on the table, a container of pens, a book by the bedside table with glasses next to them, and slippers that sat by the bed waiting for their owner to put them on when they slid out of bed. My curiosity led me to the walk-in closet on the left wall where I wondered if I would find clothing waiting for its owner as it seemed this used to be Sir Anthony's room. I swung open one of the doors of the closet and it was bigger than mine! The closet extended in and turned a corner to who knows where. Lining the wall down to the corner were suits of varying shades of gray and tweed. It reminded me of what I had read in stories of Englishmen and their grand estates. Funny to find that image here in the US and on the West Coast. You just don't see many people in suits these days. The lights showed rows of clothes, shoes, kerchiefs, hats, scarfs, and man-purses. Everything looked so exquisite. Each of these items was probably worth more than everything I owned combined. It was like I had walked into my very own mall, except I wasn't a man, so none of these items were useful to me. Continuing on around the corner a sense of wonder got hold of me. Lining the wall at the far end were ten old steamer trunks stacked on top of each other in two columns. I had always wanted one as a coffee table or one that sat at the foot of my bed, and now I owned ten of them! Each one was locked by a big padlock probably as big as my hand. Excitement got hold of me when I realized there were now eleven chests that I could explore. After some more digging around I headed out. That's when I screamed and jumped three feet into the air right when I entered the room as there was a man standing by the door, looking at me.

"You scared me half to death, Andy!" I exclaimed while gasping for air.

"I'm terribly sorry. I did not mean to startle you. I saw the door open and came in to check since the room has not been cleared out since Sir Anthony's passing and no one is allowed in, except you, of course. I did peek in the closet and noticed you, so I waited out here as I wanted to leave you space to continue exploring. If it wasn't you I was ready to use the element of surprise to stop them when they came out," Andy said.

"I wanted to explore and thought I'd start here. His closet is exquisite."

"Yes, Sir Anthony loved his material items. He collected all sorts of stuff from around the world."

Maybe there was a theme to each room. Chinese for my room, English for his room, and maybe Indian, Swedish, or Thai? Maybe I could find out what he had brought back and write an article about it.

"By the way, I found a plate of cheesecake here on the table," holding up my plate with only a couple bites out of it.

"Oh! I totally forgot about it. I hope Cook doesn't mind, but I couldn't help myself; it looked so good."

"She won't mind at all. You should sit and enjoy it."

"Why don't you show me how to get to the garden outside? I'd love to have a peek and eat my cheesecake out there."

"Are you sure you don't want to sit by the fire in the library? It's much warmer there."

"I'd like to enjoy the outdoors for a bit. Get some fresh air. I have some chests I want to go back in and explore so here's a good opportunity to get out for a while."

"As you wish. Right this way." As Andy turned, I saw a quizzical look on his face as if he was trying to figure out what I was all about.

13

ANDY SHOWED me to the terrace overlooking the back gardens. Technically, I guess this was the backyard, but it looked as big as a botanical garden in a metropolis. Big enough to host hundreds of people without feeling crowded.

"The parties here must have been out of this world."

"They used to be. They got smaller every year as people got older and grander parties were being held by the younger generation."

Andy didn't elaborate on this anymore, and I wasn't sure if I could pry more. I wanted to know everything about this house and its past owner.

"Andy, do you know anything about the chests that are in my closet and in Sir Anthony's?"

"That I could not tell you. Sir Anthony has had them in his closet since he was young. Some are from Lord Anthony and his ancestors. In the few times I helped him open them I've seen memorabilia or traveling essentials he keeps stored. I know the one in your closet was moved just seven months ago as I helped him move that one. He wanted you to have it. I could not tell you what is in it though."

My curiosity piqued even more, and I wanted to get moving in that direction to find out what was in the chest. However, since I was already here in the garden, I decided to go explore.

"Do you think the key to those chests are on the key ring you gave me?"

"Sir Anthony was a very organized man and I would be surprised if he left a key off the ring."

"Oh, that's great. I left the key ring in the library and will go do just that after I walk around a bit."

"Have a good time, and if I may make a suggestion?"

"Of course."

"I would put that key ring somewhere safer than in an area everyone can access. Some of those keys are for you only."

"Oh yes, I hadn't thought of that. Thank you, Andy."

"One last thing, Cook said she could have dinner ready in an hour if you are hungry."

"That would be fantastic. And Victoria would like to come visit. Do you think the driver could go pick her up?" Andy paused at this and it started making me uneasy that I had done something wrong.

"Don't be worried, I was just thinking of how to word this, but I don't think there's a way around it. The driver left at lunch already to go pick up your mother. She said she felt bad for not coming up with you and wanted to come meet you for dinner tonight," Andy said.

"Oh! That's fantastic! Then just two for dinner. I'll let Victoria know to take the bus up. She won't get here till very late."

I turned to look at the garden again and decided what I needed at this time was nature. Bringing my remaining cheesecake I walked down the terrace steps. The house was quiet, but every once in a while you would hear a door close or voices talking where workers were moving around cleaning or doing their own business. Here in the gardens, it was like all the sound had been absorbed into the foliage. I loved it instantly. The path in front of me took me past what looked like shrubs toward an arched opening. It looked like an open doorway to a secret garden.

Walking through brought me to a big open pasture and another walkway that led to my left and my right. Heading to my left I went through another archway. This part of the garden looked a bit darker with hedges seven feet tall lining both sides. I didn't want to go in too far as the sun was starting to set, but my curiosity wouldn't let me stop. This house got more mysterious the more I discovered. The wall started to get lower and lower the further in I walked. It also started to spiral to the right. At the end I saw a glimpse of a bench. That's when I heard my name being called from the direction of the terrace. It was almost a whisper from where I was. I walked back around the spiral and headed back up the stairs to the terrace where I found my mom looking out at the garden to the right watching the sun set in the distance.

"It's beautiful, isn't it? I'm so happy you're here!" I said as I approached her from behind and gave her a big hug.

"It's breathtaking."

"What made you decide to come?"

"You're transitioning into a new part of your life and I wanted to be a part of it. Whatever had gotten to me the other day—I let it go, and here I am."

"I love you, Mom," I said, giving her another big hug.

"I love you too, Sweetheart."

"Do you want to go in for dinner? Cook made the best fried rice today, and I'm sure her dinner will be just as tantalizing." I was met with silence, and I watched for a few seconds as my mom stared back out at the garden.

"Mom?"

"Yes, let's go in."

"Are you okay?"

"I'm fine. The garden—it reminds me of a story your Ai Po once told me. All these English gardens probably look alike."

"I found some chests I'd love to open with you if you can stay longer after dinner?"

"Yes, let's go eat."

We walked back in where Andy was waiting for us. He led us to the sitting room where I had had lunch earlier today. While we waited for dinner, I told my mom about all that had happened. She seemed to perk up when I mentioned the Asian pictures and the trunk to her but did not voice any opinions. Cook made an amazing dish of beef noodle soup in honor of my mom coming. Mom even gave it high praises—which says a lot given that Mom was an excellent cook of Chinese cuisine in her own right.

After dinner, I brought Mom straight to my room. She marveled at the carving of the tree and blossoms.

"Anne, I brought stuff to stay overnight. I'm not leaving till tomorrow. Can this wait? That dinner has made me more tired than I thought," said Mom, bewildered that something in the house had gotten me this excited.

"Mom, I just want to show you this one thing. It won't take long." I was too excited to wait till tomorrow to show her the trunk. It was all I could think about as I was this close to seeing what was inside. I sprinted through the room and into the closet with my mom trying to keep up.

"It's right through here. There are ten trunks in Sir Anthony's room, but this one is different, and Andy helped him move it into my room right before he passed away. It was meant for me. I think there's a theme to each room. Sir Anthony's is English and mine is Chinese. Mom, there's so much to discover here. It's like I've inherited a secret box, but it's a whole house."

"Look at you, getting all excited after only being in the house for one day. Don't let the wealth get to your head, you silly girl."

"I am not silly. There is a lot of history and interesting stories to be dug up here and all the rooms are so unique you can't just look at them without wishing the walls could talk."

"Be careful of where you start digging. Sometimes there are stories that are best left in the past and never dug up."

"Mom, you're being dramatic. I just thought you would appreciate finding some new things here."

"Yes, yes, show me this trunk you can't stop talking about."

I knelt in front of the trunk and pulled out the keys. There were so many that I didn't know if I would ever find out the full use of all of them. I went through the key ring one by one bursting with excitement. About three-quarters of the way through, I started getting a sinking feeling. All of these keys were regular keys. Some were very old-looking with fancy designs on them, but they still had the long stick with teeth on the end that went into a vertical jagged keyhole. None of them were H-shaped or even came close to fitting into this particular lock. Sure enough, I got to the end and none of them matched.

"I'm sorry, Anne. I really thought the key would be on the ring. It's not like Sir Anthony to not have everything in order," said Andy who had followed us in without my realizing it.

I had thought the same and had assumed everything in this house would be obtainable for me to go through at will—especially this chest that was specifically put in my room. In my excitement to finding out its content I had forgotten I had only moved in today. This chest would just have to wait. Worse case, I'd hire a locksmith to open it.

"Anne, let's go to sleep and see if there's another solution tomorrow," said Mom.

"Okay . . . Andy, thank you for your help. My mom can just sleep with me in my room for tonight."

"As you wish, but the room right next to you is already made up for her if that would be more comfortable."

"I would like that," said Mom.

"Mom, are you sure? You don't seem yourself and I know how you are in a new place, especially one so large."

"I will be fine. I have survived this long," Mom snapped at me.

"Okay, okay. I'll show you to your room."

"I will show Victoria to her room when she arrives."

"Thank you, Andy."

I showed my mom to her room, and she bid me goodnight as soon as she went in.

I spent the next couple of hours getting some things unpacked and laid in my bed thinking how much my life had changed in less than a week.

❧ 14 ☙

THE NEXT MORNING, my mom was awfully quiet through breakfast, though I could see her fascinated by the architecture in the sitting room. She had always liked plants and being in sunlight, so I thought she would really enjoy that room. Cook made congee with pork and preserved duck eggs, which we both slurped right up. *I could get used to this.*

"Anne!"

"Victoria!" I expostulated, as I ran and gave her a big hug. I was so glad she had come.

"Wait till I show you everything I've discovered."

"I can't wait, but what are you guys eating? It smells divine. Hi, Ms. Lin," she crooned, as she leaned over and gave Mom a big hug as well.

"I hear you're headed to Europe soon."

"Yes, I'm leaving tomorrow. I thought I could see Anne and then head to the airport in the morning."

"I see, so it was out of convenience more than anything else," I said giving her a joking raised eyebrow. Before she could reply, in walked Sebastian.

"Hi, Sebastian," I said, looking quite surprised to see him again so soon.

"Hi, I wanted to stop by before the week started as I found something that belongs to you."

"That belongs to me?"

"Anne, is this *the* Sebastian?" Mom asked while she and Victoria stared with wide eyes, fully turned in their seats, and very obviously checking Sebastian out. I was so embarrassed I unconsciously started slinking down into my seat.

"Hi, Ms. Lin. Yes, I'm Sebastian. It's really nice to meet you in person. And you must be Victoria. Very nice to meet you."

"The pleasure is mine," Victoria cooed making me slide even further down into my seat.

"Won't you join us for breakfast?" said Mom.

"I'm sorry, I can't today. Business calls even during the weekend. I wanted to give this to Anne. Sir Anthony had asked me to double check if all the information in the envelope was up to date and correct. This item must have fallen out when I took all the documents out, and I just found it today in the safe inside the larger envelope. I apologize because I should have been more thorough. It's not like me to miss details."

It was all I could do to keep up with how fast he was talking. He seemed to want to leave, and yet he had come to bring this object. As he was talking, I looked at the object in my hand and my heart skipped a beat. It was the key! The H-shape was undeniable as it made up the entire key and not just the endpoint. It was so simple and like nothing I had ever seen before. I wanted to go open the trunk immediately.

"No harm done. You couldn't have come at a better time. It's the key I'm looking for. Thank you for coming over."

"I'm glad I could help, but may I ask what key?" Sebastian said giving me an odd look.

"The key to the trunk I found yesterday. It should fit perfectly," I said, doing a happy dance.

"Interesting. You will have to show me the next time I come. I need to leave now." And with that, he was gone, almost at a sprint.

"What a charming fellow. Does he come here often?" Mom asked.

"Yeah Anne, does he come here often?" asked Victoria. They were both leaning on their elbows with big doe eyes looking at me with their full attention.

"No, he checks in every once in a while because Sir Anthony asked him to, but that's it."

"I remember you mentioning he had just stopped by yesterday?"

"Like he said, he found this in his drawer and said it fell out of the envelope. That's the only reason he came today."

"Okay, Anne. Okay," said Mom. I wasn't going to entertain their romantic ideas even if I couldn't get my own romantic ideas out of my head.

"Let's go open the trunk. I want to see what's inside it." I almost dragged my mom and Victoria up the stairs to my room.

We knelt down in front of the chest again, and I inserted the key. It fit perfectly, and the lock opened without any constraint. I looked at my mother and Victoria, and we all held our breath as I opened the lid.

A smell of mustiness bombarded our senses. It took a few seconds to gather my thoughts again—the smell was so strong. On the top of the trunk was a gown. It was a simple, traditional Chinese qipao of bright red silk with gold outlines of flowers adorning the dress from top to bottom. It had cap sleeves at the shoulder and two gold floral buttons (called floral pankous) one at the neck and one along the right collarbone. The dress hit below the knee. As soon as I pulled the dress out of the trunk, I heard an audible gasp from behind me. I turned to look at my mom and she had her hands over her mouth and her eyes were big and round.

"Mom, are you okay?"

"That's—that's your—I have to leave."

"Mom!" I chased her into the room and turned her around to face me.

"Mom, *what* is wrong?"

"Your Ai Po had a dress just like that."

"Ai Po? Maybe it's just a coincidence. Many people must have had this dress. It looks quite simple."

"Maybe, but it's the exact dress. I remember looking at pictures of her in that exact dress."

"Mom, I think you're over-thinking things. Why don't you come back with me and we'll see what else is in the trunk? I saw some notebooks under the gown, and that might give us a clue as to who the dress belonged to."

I knew my mom's curiosity would get the better of her, and sure enough, she came back into the closet with me. We once again knelt down in front of the trunk and I took out the top left notebook. My hands automatically tried to open it from the right and I realized it actually opened from the left. Opening to the first page I heard my mom gasp again. On the front cover of the notebook were three letters in Chinese written from top to bottom, 陳恩惠. I was a bit startled, but then again, maybe others had the same name, too, and these might not even be the same Chinese characters. I turned to look at my mom—she had tears rolling down her face.

"Mom, why are you crying?"

"Because it is *not* a coincidence. That's your Ai Po's name."

"Ai Po?" I knew her name was En-Hui Chen, but I had never seen it on any documents. The next page started with a date and continued on in first person as if the person was telling her own story just for herself—like this was a journal. I dropped the journal and stared at it. My mom was now sobbing.

"This is my Ai Po's personal journal from 1935? How have I never seen or heard anything about them before?"

"I didn't have them to give you. Most of what I learned about my mother were through her pictures, and every once in a while, she would tell me a story. I used to think she made them up to entertain me. Now I'm not so sure. But your Ai Po didn't like the past, so what I know is speculation. I'm as clueless as you on how these journals and dress got here. And it's not 1935. It's 1946."

"But it says here, 35年9月15日."

"Yes, but I know she moved here in the 40s so that must be in the Chinese calendar which has a start date of January 1, 1912. So, you add eleven to the 民 國 (Mínguó) Calendar to convert it to the Gregorian calendar."

"That's so complicated, but Mom, this is huge! You should read these journals with me and learn more about your mom."

"No, I do not want to. Good thing I sent you to all those Chinese classes growing up. You are sufficient enough to read them yourself. I'm sure the library has a dictionary to help you with the rest. This is too much for me. I am going home."

"You're going home already? I haven't even shown you the other parts of the house or the grounds."

"I do not need to see them. I am going home. I am too tired for these kinds of surprises, and remember, I grew up with your Ai Po. I do not want to relive it again."

"Mom, if only you would—"

"NO, call the car to take me home. That's the one nice thing from this whole affair. I don't have to wait on a taxi or a bus to get home."

"Okay, but I'm going to check in on you again this week."

I went out of the closet and rang for Andy. He had shown me the hidden buttons by the door of each room when I needed to get a hold of him. Somehow, he had wings on his feet as he showed up within two minutes.

"Andy, my mom wants to go home. Could you please call for the driver to take her home?"

"Yes, absolutely, but may I ask if your mom is okay? She only just arrived."

"Yes, she's fine. A bit startled by our discovery and I think she just needs some rest in her own environment." Andy seemed to perk up when I mentioned a discovery and glanced in the direction of the closet, but I didn't mention anything else, and he didn't ask.

"I will go get the driver immediately. He should be out front in ten minutes."

"Thank you, Andy."

Inside the closet, Mom was kneeling over the trunk, touching the journals. I gave her some space for a few minutes, but I knew she wanted to head home. Touching her shoulder, we both sat there for a few minutes more. Victoria was sitting on my bed to give us some space, but I could tell she was antsy to talk to me alone.

Mom turned to me with tear-ridden eyes. "Take care of them."

"I will, Mom."

With that, she got up and headed out of the room. I walked her to the car and watched as they drove away. I felt extra lonely—not sure if what I discovered was a good or bad thing. Victoria bombarded me and started talking as soon as I came in.

"Oh my god, I can't believe you found something that belonged to your Ai Po! Do you want to start reading them now? Maybe we could read them together today. I want to read, too, if that's okay? I would be really interested. But I understand if you want to keep it private."

"Slow down, Victoria," I laughed as she was five inches from my face with her hands gripping my arms. "Yes, you can read with me. It'll be nice to not be alone." There was a new mystery to find out. Why were my Ai Po's journals in this house?

❦ 15 ❦

I WENT BACK to the closet and looked at the trunk. Something told me there was no turning back once I started, and my curiosity definitely wouldn't let this rest. So, I picked up the first journal, put the gown back in the trunk, and went with Victoria to the library downstairs. I was at least going to be comfortable.

Somehow, Andy knew I would be using the room that day as the fire was burning when I got in. The Chinese dictionary was right where all the reference books were. I settled myself on the sofa next to Victoria, covered the both of us with a blanket, took a deep breath, and opened to the first page.

35年9月15日 (Sunday, September 15, 1946)

I'm so glad I have you, Journal. I don't know how I will get through this new change in my life without you. My parents told me this morning that we are moving to America next week. Yeah, I agree, why am I only finding out about this now? Apparently, they had been planning this the whole year and didn't want me to get too anxious until plans were formalized. As a child, I only "needed to know." I'm seventeen, for goodness' sake, but of course, this means nothing. I still live under my father's roof and hence I do as I'm told.

I wonder if American kids follow these same rules. Aunt Ruby is a distant cousin of my parents. She was willing to help us move to America. She was born and raised in the US, as were her parents, and her parents before that. I lost track of how we were related but basically, her ancestors were able to get into the US before 1882 when the Chinese Exclusion Act was put into effect. They probably went over during the Gold Rush or when the railroads were being built. Her family ran a successful garment store in California. The Exclusion Act was repealed three years ago, and unbeknownst to me, my parents had been looking for a way to move over. With only 105 spots for Chinese immigrants, she had pulled every string she had to get papers for us. Sentiments toward the Chinese were still not great, so she told us how to act, what to say, and not to say in front of the Americans. We're some of the lucky ones and have an actual family member willing to help. We've heard horror stories of people going to America with false papers being treated brutally and being sent back. Opportunities are supposed to be bountiful in America, and my parents say I will have a better life and more opportunities than staying in Taiwan. I don't know. I will miss our life here and all of my friends and family. I might not see Ai Po again. The thought of moving to a country where we aren't very welcome scares me half to death, but I have no say in the move, and my parents have always known best. Let's hope I will be able to make some friends. I hate being alone.

35年9月22日 (Sunday, September 22, 1946)

Oh my goodness. This cannot be happening. My parents have told me that when we arrive in America that I will be moving in with a very wealthy family to be their personal seamstress, cook, cleaner, whatever they need me to do. Work I can deal with. I've sewed, cooked, cleaned, and done many jobs since I could manage by myself, but my parents will not be joining me at the house! They said we were all supposed to be in San Francisco with my aunt working at her garment factory, but this opportunity came up in Portland, Oregon, and they wanted someone young who could grow with the family. The pay was too good to say no to, and my aunt really talked me up. I am a very good seamstress and cook, and yes, I had been mentioning I wanted more freedom from my parents, but we're going to be in a totally new country and they won't be there with me! My English is very rudimentary, and I was sure the family knew no Chinese. They said they did not want to worry me before we left, but I don't think I can take any more surprises. We are on this big boat, and I'm seasick and fretting that I am going to be away from everyone and everything I know. I don't understand why this is happening. We did not have a lot of money in Taiwan, but we lived a simple life. Breathe . . . I need to keep breathing.

35年9月29日 (Sunday, September 29, 1946)

I hate boats. I never want to get on a boat again. I have thrown up more times than I wish to count. I...WANT...TO...GET...OFF!

35年10月6日 (Sunday, October 6, 1946)

It's been two weeks at sea. My parents aren't doing so well themselves. They haven't thrown up as much as me, but they have agreed that the view has gotten quite boring and the food is subpar. We're all miserable down in the bottom of the boat and ready for dry land. Have I mentioned that I hate boats? We're supposed to be at a port in three days, and we cannot wait to get off. At this point, I don't care where I go. I just want to get off this boat!

35年10月9日 Wednesday, October 9, 1946

LAND! We are on flat land again. It was a good thing we were so prepared because the questioning through immigration was brutal. I am not a good liar and if we had fake papers, I would have had to get back on that boat. That was my worst fear. The humiliation to my family would be unbearable, too, after all the work they put into getting us here. The eyes of the people who interviewed us were mean. You could tell they were looking for any fault they could find. I am not looking forward to this new country. We could tell they were making fun of us even though we couldn't understand every word they said. I won't let them bring me down, though. I will make my family proud. I will just be scared doing it.

35年10月11日 (Friday, October 11, 1946)

We saw Aunt Ruby, toured her factory, which was much bigger than what we had in Taiwan, and left the next day to go up to Portland. The family was anxious for me to start working. The drive up was so beautiful. We followed the ocean all the way up. I grew up on an island, but we never went to the ocean a lot. Because I wasn't on the boat anymore, I enjoyed this trip so much more. Green scenery on the right and ocean on the left. When we got deeper into Oregon, the lusciousness of the trees enveloped us, and we kept driving through a dewy mist. It was green everywhere, even when we drove inland toward Portland. We stayed at a friend's place in the city. She also owned a garment store, and for the whole night, I imagined what my new place of work would look like, what the people would be like, would I be liked? And I listened to some of the machines still working downstairs. My employer sent their driver to come pick us up where we were staying. I remembered the driver having a startled look when he saw us, but he clearly was a professional as his face went neutral within a second of seeing me stare at him. We drove up into the hills, and I was not expecting what I saw when we showed up at the house. We had to call through an intercom, they had to open the gate, and we drove up a road lined with trees on both sides. Everything was cut to exact dimensions, and it looked like someone punched out the trees, bushes, grass, and road from a paper cut-out and placed it in its exact location. Everything was so pristine, it was a little disturbing. How does someone have so much money and own so much property?! I had not seen this amount of property in Taiwan. Then again, I never ventured too far from my area.

My parents were quite impressed by my new working environment and maybe a tad jealous. Serves them right for leaving me here alone. We approached a roundabout, and a fountain was in the middle surrounded by roses of all different colors. The door was so large I kept staring at it even when it opened, and I had to look down to see who opened the door. A boy younger than me stared at us with quizzical eyes. He was in a suit and looked as if he worked here. He ushered us in, and we stood at the entrance ogling the massiveness of the entryway.

Chandeliers hung from the ceiling and gave a pleasant glow to the house. Very soon after the boy left—who we later found to be called Andy—a lady dressed in a blue shirtwaist dress, buttons down the front, and a simple blue belt around her waist came walking in. She was poised and elegant, and I couldn't take my eyes off of her. She had little pearl studs in her ears and her hair was curly and swept up on the top of her head. She addressed us in Chinese, which for a Westerner was pretty good. She switched back to English quickly, but I must have dropped my mouth open because the next thing I knew, my mom was elbowing me. I still have a bruise—that's how hard she elbowed me. I could have stared at her all day. I remember standing up straighter and wanting to impress her—not like me at all. She said she was the lady of the house and showed us around—library, kitchen, and my room, which had a sitting area with a bedroom in the back.

The sitting area was where I would do my work. We learned that she used to be an avid dresser and frequently entertained. Now that the war was over and the limitations on what women and men could wear were lifted, she wanted to get back as much as she could. Hence, where I came in. She wanted to take down her old dresses that were saved from the war and make new dresses for her and her daughters. She had also obtained new cloth of brighter colors and wanted to make more dresses that had more materials on the bottom and weren't so form-fitting. They would be looser, like before the war, and leave the men guessing, as she put it. Occasionally, she would ask for new suits for her husband and sons, but in the meantime, if I could take the wartime jackets and make them into more casual wear, that would be my job after finishing the girls' outfits. She had all the patterns I needed and expected me to start immediately. She mentioned that they bought a lot of ready-made outfits now, too, so eventually, I would be helping Marjorie in the kitchen, and others around the house. She seemed nice enough, but time will tell. I was extremely sad after this as my parents left soon after. The lady guaranteed I would be in good hands, and I was allowed to go see my parents once a year. I was to be paid monthly, and I told my parents I would send the money on to them as soon as I got it.

My finger rubbed the bottom right corner of the paper where it was wrinkled, and I could imagine my Ai Po crying as she wrote this. I felt for her, but more so, I was overwhelmed by the information I was learning about her. She lived here. In this exact house. I didn't know if I should be happy to have finally found these journals or if I should be mad for them being hidden all this time. This was my family history, not the Wilkens' even if she did work for them. They had no right to hang on to these journals. Most of the times I asked my mom about her I was met with silence. What she did share was I had only met her twice when I was an infant and when I was two. She passed away the year after. At that time, she was already in a nursing home. My mom would go every week to see her, which I believe was more out of obligation than anything else, but she wouldn't bring me. I never thought anything of her as she was not a part of my life, but I remembered being jealous of my classmates who would go on vacation to visit their grandparents. I secretly wanted to tag along, and yet I also didn't understand what the big deal was about going to see grandparents. Here in front of me was a real-life person telling me her story. I could not wait to read more. Plus, my head was hurting from translating. Victoria had been holding my arm, and we were leaning against each other, but she stayed quiet to allow me to continue with my thoughts.

Lavender had come in and dropped off some small sandwiches for lunch, which I was very appreciative of. I closed the journal gently and brought it back to my room where I put it in the desk drawer for safekeeping. A walk would do me good, and my thoughts went immediately to the bench I saw a glimpse of yesterday.

❦ 16 ❦

THE COLD AIR brought me right back to the present. I breathed deeply and headed toward the spiral I walked through. The bench was inviting, and it was nice to have my own private space to relax outdoors. We approached the bench and noticed an inscription on the top: "To my two loves who are always in my heart." There was a plum blossom on either side of the inscription. Then, we turned around and saw the most bewildering scene in front of us.

"Why do you think that was made?" asked Victoria.

"I can't imagine, but it's so well done. You can see his expression shine through."

The bench was out in the open in a big space and faced back toward where I came in from. Right by the entrance was a small statue of a little boy chasing butterflies. His arms were raised up, his legs were in mid-jump, and he had the happiest look on his face. He couldn't be more than two or three years old. Around him were toys that he would have been playing with before chasing after the butterflies. Blocks, trains, trucks, and books. Everything was spread over a stone blanket. I wasn't sure what to make of it and wondered who had asked for this to be made or placed here. What was their infatuation with children? I breathed the cool air in and out—watching the condensation float away. The last two days had raised more questions than answers. My Ai Po actually lived here. But why would I inherit this house? It made no sense.

"I have to head to the airport soon."

"The weekend went by too fast. When am I going to see you next?"

"I don't know. I have no set time for this trip. I'm just going to see where it goes."

"Remind me where you're going again?"

"Germany, then Italy, then Switzerland, and then hopefully Spain, Britain, Scotland, and from there I'm going to decide if I've had enough or move on to other countries or a different continent."

"That sounds so nice. I wish I had taken you up on your offer for me to join."

"You still can, but I know you and you can't walk away from this new life of yours just yet. I want full updates on what you discover about your Ai Po. My parents gave me a cell phone with an international plan. I'm to only use it in emergencies, but I'm still to call them at least once a month. I expect to talk to you once a month, too."

"Oh, that would be great! I was going to suggest I could pay for it, but I didn't want you to think that I was just going to start throwing money at every situation."

Someone coughed, and I looked toward the entrance. Sebastian was standing there looking at me, and I felt my face go red. I was lucky I was in so many layers as the rest of my body was probably just as red.

"Why hello," I said "two days in a row and twice today. If I didn't know any better, I'd say you were keeping tabs on me." *Where do I come up with this stuff?*

"Very funny," but I saw him blush even under the already pink cheeks. He looked awkward standing there and seemed to not know what to do next.

"Well, this is my cue to leave," Victoria said as she started toward the entrance, turning back only to give me a wink. I tried to stop her so that I wasn't left alone, but she was uncatchable. "I'll see you soon, Anne. Enjoy your time here," and with that, she was gone.

"Your friend is quite a vibrant character."

"You mean her clothes or her personality?"

"Both. I can see how you two are friends."

"You can?" I asked, looking at him skeptically.

"Opposites attract. Isn't that how it always works?"

"Um—sure. Want to sit? Did you know about this statue?"

"Yes, they're all over the property. Sir Anthony had them commissioned in the 60s. I'm not sure why. The statues are usually a kid of varying age."

"Varying age?"

"Sir Anthony explained to me that it's of one kid, and he 'grows' as you go around the property. It's really quite amazing the amount of detail he put into it. Andy said that it was one of his life projects, but I never could get any details from either of them. I do know he was an avid contributor to the Children's Hospital. He seemed to have a genuine love for children. It might stem from the fact that he and Sally were never able to have children."

"Sir Anthony and Andy seemed quite close. And who was Sally?"

"They were. Very close. Sally was his wife, and she passed away over fifteen years ago from cancer. Some staff members would tell you it was out of sadness, but I couldn't get much detail from anyone. Andy was six years younger than Sir Anthony, but Sir Anthony was his favorite out of all the siblings, and he devoted himself to Sir Anthony for the rest of his life. They are each other's closest confidants. It's really something quite special, and sometimes I look on with envy. I've never had anyone close to talk to."

"Ha, with your looks you could charm a fish right out of a bear's mouth." *Drat, why in the world did I just say that? It probably didn't even make any sense.*

There was an awkward silence, and I noticed him looking around —probably trying to figure out a way to escape.

Breaking the silence, he said, "I'm not sure why I'm here, but you mentioned the object I brought this morning was a key. I haven't been able to stop thinking about that as it was like no key I have ever seen before. I'm curious where it led to and if you found anything interesting. You seemed to be excited about it, and I just couldn't stop thinking about you—I mean *it*. You were so happy. I'm curious as to what you found."

Again, it was all I could do to keep up with the flood of words coming out of his mouth. It seemed he was genuinely interested in seeing where the key led and had I heard him slip up and say he was thinking about *me*? He seemed to be an intimate part of Sir Anthony's life and Andy always seemed comfortable with him, so what harm would it do to show him the journals?

"I found my Ai Po's journals."

Silence.

"I'm confused. Your Ai Po's journals? Who's Ai Po?"

"Oh, sorry. Ai Po is Haka for my mom's mom. In other words, my Grandmother."

"Okay, that is definitely not what I expected."

"Here, come with me. I'll show you."

I took one last look at the little boy and smiled. He looked so happy. I made a note to explore the rest of the garden tomorrow.

SEBASTIAN and I sat in the closet while I translated the portion I had read earlier. I kept making mistakes I was so nervous to see what he thought. The guy didn't even know Ai Po and had never known us, so I don't know why I put so much weight on his opinion. I just had no one else to talk to.

"That was . . . Amazing. I would have never thought your Ai Po lived in this very house. That still doesn't explain why you inherited the house, but it is definitely helping us solve the mystery."

"I'm still digesting it all. I'm not sure what to think as I never knew my Ai Po. My mom saw the journals and fled! She told me she couldn't support me at this time and my best friend just left for Europe," I said as I started walking fast around the room. I felt trapped and frustrated. All of this family history had just been sitting in this old man's house and the only reason we had found it was because he died and was kind enough to give it to us. Not exactly how I had pictured learning my family history.

"Hey, breathe," said Sebastian as he grabbed my arms and made me stop pacing. "You're acting like a trapped animal, and it's making me nervous. I smelled something delicious coming from the kitchen when I arrived and I bet Cook is prepping dinner."

"Lavender teased me this afternoon that Cook is making a lamb dish tonight, and I'm starving. Do you want to join?" I looked at him, hoping he would stay as I could use some company.

"Sure, I'd love to join," though he seemed to check himself while saying it.

We walked down into the kitchen and saw Cook and her staff cooking away and the smell was tantalizing.

"Ah, here you are," Cook said when she spotted us. "Come, come. Come taste my lamb stew. I think you will like it very much."

Who were we to say no to an open invitation? A set of two plates was set up at the table and Cook served us a good helping of lamb stew that I devoured and requested more. That pleased her to no end. Sebastian was not far behind with his second helping, too. While we ate, I noticed Cook looking at us, and I wondered how long she had been here. She looked about the same age as Andy and I wondered if she was here when Ai Po was here.

"Cook, can we ask you some questions?"

"Of course, ask away."

"When did you start working here?"

"I came around the same time as Andy, though I was five years older. Lord and Lady Wilkens wanted to revitalize their staff and hired us young folks to train to their liking. My mom was a wonderful cook and taught me everything she knew. At fifteen, I started cooking for catering services that catered rich people's galas and word got around that I was the one to hire. I was hired here a year later and never left. I am still the best cook amongst my peers and proud of it."

Sebastian and I nodded in agreement. I had never eaten so well in my life. Food would magically appear and be divine.

"The house was bustling in those days. Lots of guests and dinner parties. They loved to throw a big gala at the end of the year as well. Sir Anthony kept it up for a while, but I think he did it more out of tradition. His health was not so good the last several years."

"Cook, do you remember a Chinese girl being hired here as a seamstress?"

"Oh, I do. She was a lovely girl. She joined shortly after I did.

Andy, she, and I called ourselves the Three Musketeers. Rose had found the book in the library and we all loved it." She was silent for a bit—lost in her own thoughts and then, "I should go check on dessert. Would you two like dessert?"

"We would love some. Rose?" and before I could ask her more, Cook had walked off.

"She does like to talk, that's for sure," said Sebastian.

"Yeah, but I wonder why she stopped sharing all of a sudden."

"Cook has always been scattered and I'm sure she just wanted to go check on her dessert. She's very proud of her dishes if you didn't notice already. Maybe it was close to being done."

We waited a solid twenty minutes before Cook came back. When she did, she was carrying two slices of rum cake and they were mouthwatering. When I bit into the cake, it was light and spongy while the rum flowed down my throat warming me from the inside out. I could really get used to this, but boy, did I need to start exercising again.

"How do you like my rum cake?" asked Cook, looking at us with a 'dare say it's no good and I will be mad' look.

"It's delicious," and I was glad I did not have to lie. I asked for seconds on this, too.

"Cook, before you go, could you tell us a bit more . . . ?"

"Oh dear, the pots are overflowing. I must go tend to them. You two enjoy your cake. There will be more delicious food tomorrow."

"That was definitely a diversion. There are no overflowing pots, and her staff would take care of it, too," I huffed.

"Let's go find Andy. Maybe he will shed some light on what you've found."

Sebastian led me to Andy's room (before I could cause a scene), which was right down the hallway behind the library. I bet it was so he could hear the front door if needed. Andy was looking through some papers when we walked in.

"Ah, Sebastian and Anne. Please do sit down. Is there something you need?"

"Andy, I found my Grandmother's dress and journals in the chest we tried to open last night. It seemed she worked here and Cook just said the three of you arrived around the same time. I wanted to ask—"

"Anne, I need to stop you there. Cook never knows when to hold her tongue, so take her words with a grain of salt, but yes, the three of us arrived around the same time, and we did know your Grandmother Rose. I was not to say anything to you per Sir Anthony's wishes. Your Grandmother was a lovely person, and since you have found her journals, I will let her tell you her story herself. After you have read them, if you still have questions then you can come to me. I will share what I know, but that is all I can say."

In shock, I stood there and stared at Andy while growing red in the face and ready to hurl something. I had never felt this mad before, not even when Brian dumped me. This guy's house was given to me without any notice, which made Mom start acting weird, opened up a mystery about my Ai Po who I never knew, and the people who knew her best wouldn't talk. AAHH!

"Anne, I think we should go. Let's go to the garden."

"Why won't you tell me anything?" I yelled at Andy who was trying not to look at me.

"I cannot. I must do as Sir Anthony wishes."

"He's dead! He's not here anymore. Neither is my grandmother who I never knew!"

"I cannot. I'm sorry."

Sebastian dragged me out of the office and down the hallway. He held onto me as I seethed and walked out onto the balcony overlooking the garden. We kept walking until we got to the bench. Luckily, he at least had the sense to grab our coats on our way past the entrance. I burrowed into my coat and just stared at the happy little boy wondering why all the secrecy. Why didn't anyone say things out right?

"Andy has worked here for decades. This is the only life he knows, and I knew Sir Anthony. He was very good to the staff, and they loved him. They were very loyal to him and it doesn't surprise me that they are still loyal even after his death, especially Andy and

Cook. You have the journals and it seemed like there were quite a few in the trunk. Read some more tomorrow and I can stop by again as well."

I turned and looked at Sebastian. "Why are you being so nice to me? Do you have a secret, too or something to gain?"

"No, Sir Anthony asked me to check in on you and maybe I'm doing it too much. I don't have to come tomorrow."

"No, it would be nice to have someone to share these journals with. I'm upset. I never knew my grandmother, and all of a sudden I'm in possession of some of her most intimate things. I'm learning about her, and all these secrets are popping up, and I have no one to share them with or talk it out with. I'm confused and frustrated."

"Well, let's call it a night and I'll see you tomorrow," said Sebastian. He gave me a light kiss on my forehead, and with that, he got up and started walking toward the entrance. He seemed to pause as if he knew what he just did was odd, but he kept walking. I was a bit startled by the kiss, but it warmed me up on the inside. At least it seemed I had made a new friend if not one who felt obligated to come and check up on me. At least it was someone to talk to.

❦ 18 ❦

SLEEP EVADED ME THAT NIGHT. I kept thinking about Ai Po at the doorstep of this house. Alone when her parents left. After breakfast, I found myself back in the library. My bedroom cushions lined the floor of the library by the fire. The sofa was great, but it was so much more comfortable to be closer to the fire. I opened up where I left off.

35年10月11日 (Continuation of Friday, October 11, 1946)

Andy was tasked to show me back to my room. In the time we had shown my parents to the door someone had already brought a three-foot pile of cloth in the sitting room. Next to them were designs that Lady wanted done by next week! You are my only friend here now. I have no one, and I can only understand a small portion of what they are all saying. I sat and cried until Andy came by again. He brought me some food. He called them milk and 'kra-kers.' The milk did not agree with me, but the crackers were buttery and flaky. I'd never had anything like them before. He sat next to me, didn't touch me, didn't hug me, or say anything, but waited till I calmed down. After I dried my tears, he took the tray and cup and left. I cried some more in the middle of the night, but there was some comfort in his sitting there. I didn't do any sewing today.

35年10月12日 (Saturday, October 12, 1946)

I woke up before the sun with swollen eyes from all the crying last night. The sight of my new room made me start crying all over again. I had told myself I would allow crying for the first night, and in the morning, I would get to work to make my parents proud. But secretly, I had hoped the morning would never come. Today ended up being a productive day though because after looking at the designs they were very simple dresses, and she basically wanted the same dress made out of all the different materials with some details changed here and there. I was able to outline and cut out all the pieces and set them aside today. Pat on my back, a job well done! Nothing would stop me. At least that's what I used to chant to myself when my parents gave me impossible tasks to do for the village we lived in. The garments I used to have to sew for the elders were painstakingly detailed. I saw no reason to stop chanting it now. At lunch, I did take a break, and I met Marjorie when I went searching for some food. I bumped into her in the hallway and boy, is she a talker. She also had bright red hair. It looked like her hair was on fire, and I thought I had encountered a witch! I liked her immediately. She was so happy to see another girl that was about her same age that she grabbed me by the arm and basically dragged me into the kitchen. In Taiwan, we did not physically hug or touch people very often. It was weird to have someone holding my arm, giving me what she called 'bear hugs' while talking non-stop. I only caught a word here or there. But she looked so happy and served me the most delicious food I had ever eaten. There was creamy soup filled with fish and something she called 'pork chops' that had some grainy semi-sweet yellow sauce next to it. It was all sorts of new tastes and smells. Perfect for the cold days. Eventually, I got back to my room and I've been sitting on my bed ever since. I think I made my second friend.

35年10月13日 (Sunday, October 13, 1946)

I woke up to A LOT of bustling all over the house today. Andy told me the master's son had just called this morning and said he was coming home tomorrow afternoon. Apparently, this was a last-minute visit. I saw servants flying everywhere. Taking sheets to and from a room on the second floor. I walked by to check it out and was shocked by what I saw. Full decorations for the room were being taken down and new decorations were being put up. It was like a remodeling of a room but in super-fast speed at a scale I had never seen before. New lamps, draperies, pictures, tables, and chairs were all being changed out. One of the ladies that passed through the door said that Lord Wilkens' son's taste changed every year and his mom always wanted his room prepped just right for him. Spoiled brat. I stayed in my room the rest of the day and worked on the dresses.

35年10月14日 (Monday, October 14, 1946)

Well, today was quite eventful. I woke up to rude pounding on my door. It must have been pretty hard because I have been sleeping like a log since I arrived. The time change is awful. It was Andy and Marjorie, they needed me in the kitchen to help prep the food for today. After finishing that task, they needed an extra pair of hands upstairs to finish up Sir Anthony's room before he arrived this afternoon. I was dragged into the room by the head maid and told to start dusting every square inch. If I could see it, it needed to be dusted. I danced around the other maids, dusting away, thinking I never wanted to own this many useless items if I had to clean them continuously. I watched them remake the bed for the fourth time. The first one had a stain, the other was too small, and the next was not the right color. What really fascinated me were all the different layers that went into the bed. There was the mattress cover, which I was familiar with, but then there was what they called a flat sheet that went over that and got tucked at the foot of the bed. Then there was another layer on top of that of what I think was fur, and then there was a comforter on top of that. Then the pillows. There were two regular looking pillows. Then there were two big royal blue ones, then two smaller royal blue ones that had white stripes on them. Then there were two smaller white pillows. What in the world did one person do with all those sheets and pillows? I had always had a mattress cover, one pillow, and one blanket. That was it. Everyone else I knew had the same so I don't think it was just our family. I was sent into the closet to keep dusting as I kept stopping to stare and not work. I felt sorry for the maid who had to clean all those sheets and blankets.

Shortly after, a gasp came from the main room. When I peeked out, I saw a man standing at the entrance looking around but not really noticing any of the maids. The maids, in turn, were wide-eyed, open-mouthed, and tripping over themselves. It was disgusting to see. He was blond with green eyes. His nose pointed out as if always aiming for something. And he stood there with such a presence. Then he looked at *me*. He stared at me for what seemed like an eternity and I could feel the jealous eyes of the other maids on me. I could also feel my heart beating faster and my legs start to wobble. He was handsome, but really? What had gotten into me? He was the son of the master of the house and clearly, the untouchable eye candy everyone wanted. I broke the stare first and went back to dusting in the closet as fast as I could so I could quickly excuse myself. His eyes followed me when I left. I think the head maid yelled something at me, but I couldn't have cared less. I had never reacted like that to any boy. It made me feel uncomfortable. I decided the best way to distract myself was to go visit Marjorie. Marjorie said she was going to make cake today, and I had never had an American cake before. I was very much looking forward to trying more of this American cuisine, especially if it got my mind off of Sir Anthony Wilkens.

Can't blame a girl for having a crush on a handsome rich guy. That was the last entry of the journal and my brain was tired from translating. Some parts I skipped because I couldn't decipher the words correctly, and there were areas where I filled in the blank as best I could. I hadn't had to translate whole novels since college. I was very much out of practice, but Mom would be proud as I was picking it up the more I read.

Thank goodness I found a Chinese dictionary in the library as there were many words that I didn't know. Some entries were just a couple sentences of uneventful happenings. She tried a different cake from Cook, or she went for a walk around the garden, but all the talk about Cook's food made me want to go grab lunch. I realized I had nibbled a granola bar I found in my purse for breakfast and that was it. The fridge was packed like before, but I immediately saw the chocolate cake. Who needed a nutritious meal?

"Yeah, that's what I went for, too."

I probably jumped three feet into the air and almost dropped the chocolate cake on the floor. I put it on the counter and turned toward the table. There, eating his slice of chocolate cake was Sebastian.

"What are you *doing* down here?"

"You looked so absorbed in the library I didn't want to bother you, and I knew Cook always kept a cake in the fridge and sure enough—" he held up the fork with his bite of cake on it to show me before shoving it into his mouth. I sliced a piece for myself and joined him at the table.

"I just finished reading more of my grandmother's journal, and it seemed like Sir Anthony was quite the man every girl wanted back in the day."

"I've heard from Andy and Cook that he definitely had his pick of girls to go out with and eventually marry."

"How come he never had kids?"

"Sally couldn't. They tried and eventually just gave up. I don't really know any details into that. By the way, do you mind if I read more of the journals as well? I couldn't work today I was so curious, but I wanted to ask you beforehand. Of course, if you don't want me to I won't push the matter. I just thought since you let me read the beginning . . ."

"Yes, yes, you can," I said, half laughing. It was like he was trying to be polite and extremely curious all at the same time. "I just finished the first journal and was about to start the next one.

Let's bring these cakes up to the library as I left everything as is upstairs."

"Right behind you."

We grabbed a corner of the fireplace and I picked up the journal to start reading. I looked at Sebastian a second longer than I probably should have, but it really was nice that he wanted to be here and share this with me. I'm glad I wasn't doing all of this alone. I looked at the inside cover of the second journal and there were letters written in it as if a child was practicing their ABCs. I imagined Ai Po practicing in secret in her bedroom. I ran my hands over the lettering wishing I could have met her more.

35年10月16日 (Wednesday, October 16, 1946)

It's been a couple days since I've written. The weirdest thing has happened. Sir Anthony has visited me twice in my workroom and stopped me in the hall once to ask me a question. Why me, of all people, I have no idea. None of his other siblings have visited. They've walked by and looked in like I was a zoo animal, but they've never come in or tried to talk to me. I'm not even acknowledged when I'm passed by in the hallway. That would go for the family and the staff. When he visited, I didn't even really know what he was asking. He kept pointing to my work and saying 'what dresses?' so I figured I'd show him his mother and sisters' dress designs and the cloth I was using to make them. He seemed very complimentary of my work and actually seemed interested because he kept smiling and nodding his head, but who knows?

He said a bunch of other stuff, and I just smiled and nodded. He's a very good actor if he didn't like what he saw. I thought he was a spy for his family after the first time around, so I threw myself into work to show that I was dedicated to my new job and the family, but I'm starting to think that isn't it. Cook and Andy seem to have had visits by him as well, so maybe it's not so odd. I'm used to being in the background, so to have the master's son coming to my room instead of sending someone and actually being inquisitive is so odd. Maybe they just do things differently here in America. I have so much to learn. I just hope I am not offending anyone. I've been trying to copy the other staff members in their mannerisms and habits. The staff uniform is quite scratchy and blah. White and black. I miss my qipao, which had at least some color to it and I had sewed small flowers to it to create simple designs in the corners. It was unique. Andy has also started teaching me my letters and I've memorized about half of them.

35年10月17日 (Thursday, October 17, 1946)

He came again! This time he brought a Chinese-English dictionary. Where in the world he got that, I have no idea, but I felt just a little more relaxed seeing it and seeing him try. Just a little. I tried so hard not to laugh because when he spoke 'Chinese' I couldn't understand a word he said. At one point, he stopped and stared at me and I just nodded furiously. Who knows what I was saying yes to! He seemed to laugh at himself, but I was too scared to make sure. I kept looking at my work and only sometimes glanced up to see what he would point at. He finally left after who knows how long and I breathed again. What was he up to?

The highlight of my day was seeing the plum-blossom tree and the rose bushes. I had been drawing plum blossoms the other day as they are my favorite. I have always been in awe of their hopeful perseverance as they withstand the cold of winter when they bloom. They are also beautiful and pure to behold. Andy saw me drawing, and he took me to see the new garden that was being created. Lord Anthony was redesigning the gardens to have maze-like characteristics throughout the whole backyard with roses lining the paths, and a big plum blossom tree in one of the sections. When I say backyard, I really mean 'country of its own.' I walked for thirty minutes yesterday and I barely saw even a corner of the garden. The tree was young, and I talked to it, letting it know I couldn't wait to see it blossom later in the winter. The gardener laughed at me, but it was one of those fatherly, friendly laughs. I bet he does the same thing, too. All flower lovers do.

35年10月20日 (Sunday, October 20, 1946)

Sir Anthony has come back every day. I'm no longer surprised, and his Chinese is improving though I still can't understand everything. It couldn't just be his tutor as I've met his tutor in the hallway, and he's tried to talk to me, and yes, he can speak Chinese, but boy is it broken. He must be teaching the grammar and structure to Sir Anthony and not the actual spoken language. He seems to enjoy his time with me, and I'm privately smiling inside that he wants to be here. Though I have seen him spending time with Cook and Andy as well. It seems he's trying to get to know the new staff and understand who we are and what we do. I think that's very progressive and outstanding in a boss. The idea of a boy in my room—especially one as handsome as Sir Anthony—I can live with for a while. We've developed our own way of communicating with words we know, like hello, sit, leave, yes, and no. But we also use hand gestures and pictures. I found my mao bi and drew images of what I'm trying to say on parchment paper and he has done the same. It's quite fun.

35年10月27日 (Sunday, October 27, 1946)

I'm sorry I have been neglecting you. My dread has been uplifted since moving here. I feel like I have friends and am starting to learn their language. Sir Anthony visits me every day and teaches me a few new words. Andy and Cook have been teaching me as well. So far, I've learned kitchen, library—house I already knew—mansion, the parts of dresses, food items—my favorite is cheesecake. Cheese —this is my new fascination with this country, what a variety of cheeses there are! How can I try all of them? I've tried brie, blue cheese, goat—not a fan of that one, and Gouda. I've learned different flower names such as rose, tulip, daffodils—which I love the sound of. It makes me imagine the flowers dancing in the wind. Sir Anthony seems very adamant about me learning English and in turn has fired his tutor and persuaded his parents to have me teach him Chinese. Seeing how I'm already the hired help and will not cost extra, though I think I should be paid more, they didn't think twice to make the switch.

The days here are crisp, but the air is so clean we walk through the garden to do our lessons. Usually, we end up at my favorite bench-spot which has the most privacy so no one else will hear my broken English, and more importantly, no one will hear his broken Chinese. The path to the bench spirals in on itself and has beautiful red roses lining it. The smell awakens me as I walk past all of them. Andy and Cook have told me in one way or another that this setup of mine is not a good idea. No good comes from befriending the boss. But I do not have my parents around, I'm learning English, and I have friends. I am happy for once. I learned that Sir Anthony is here for a month and then his father is sending him to Asia to look at opportunities for expanding their business. I'm not sure what they do, but he drew a picture of him standing in the US and a boat traveling to China, first with him on it, and then one boat holding a lot of items. I told him he should check out Taiwan as there were a lot of opportunities there that I didn't believe people knew about yet. I had my first snowball fight the other day, and wow, did my cheek sting. We were laughing so hard we collapsed halfway through throwing, and just looked up at the sky while watching the clouds float by. We touched fingers in the snow and I smiled for the rest of the day. I even managed to get all of Lady Mary's and her daughters' dresses finished. They wore them out last night to a ball one of their neighbors was throwing. They came back and each of them gave me a hug, including Lady Mary. I knew I had done a great job on the dress as Lady Mary usually only gives me a smile or a few words and walks away. Lord Anthony just gave me a nod, but I'll take that. He doesn't seem the acknowledging type. I'm also very scared of him.

The next few entries in the following week were about the same. My mom always kept roses in the kitchen. She would get fresh ones every weekend. She said grandma would do the same. It was kind of cool to learn where the love of roses came from. All of a sudden I wanted to go get roses to decorate my room. It would be the perfect trip after not leaving the house for the last three days. I closed the journal and looked up to see Sebastian looking at me. He was just gazing at me, and I blushed. I was so warm and comfortable in my blanket, the sun had set already, and the fire glowed perfectly on his features and made his eyes shine extra bright.

"How are you feeling?" Sebastian asked.

"I feel privileged and overwhelmed that I get to learn so much about my grandmother. It's starting to make some things make more sense about how my mom brought me up and the little things she did around the house. For example, I just read about the roses she loved while living here and my mom has always had roses in the house, and she said Ai Po did, too. It's filling in little blanks in my life and makes me feel more connected to my past."

"That's great," he said with a chuckle.

"Why are you laughing?"

"I'm not laughing. I'm smiling and happy for you. You are so serious most of the time I see you. It's nice to see you excited, and it's nice to see you reconnecting with your family even if it is through a journal. I never had a good parental figure in my life until Sir Anthony. My dad left when I was born and my mom did the best she could, but she was only eighteen and didn't really want a kid. Anyway, your mom seems great and your grandmother seems like a fascinating person. I bet she's who you get your spunk from."

"Tell me more about your childhood."

"Why don't I get you out of this house and show you some different scenery for a change. I can tell you over dinner."

I wasn't expecting to be asked to go for dinner, and we both sat there not saying anything for a few seconds.

"You can say no, too. I wouldn't be offended. Isabella had asked if I was free for dinner, and I said no as I didn't want to talk about business tonight. I just thought you could use a change of scenery. I'll give you some space and say goodnight now." Sebastian said quickly, looking away from me.

I thought it odd he would bring up Isabella, but I brushed it aside as he looked so rejected. "No, no, please stay. I'd love to go to dinner with you tonight. You caught me by surprise, and I didn't know what to say for a second. That's all. I'd like to go get roses in town so it'll save me a trip, too."

"Then it's a date. I'll drive," he said as his face lit up. We drove all the way into town and went to a restaurant he raved about the whole way there. It was called Pok Pok and the Thai food was supposed to be world-famous. I was skeptical as friends had told me there was no Thai food in the US that rivaled the original in Thailand. But Sebastian swore the food was to die for. He came here at least once a week and had never steered anyone wrong. I was always up to trying new places and I was looking forward to a change in scenery. At the first sight, I immediately loved the place. It was a converted home, and everything looked and smelled delicious. We ordered the fish sauce wings, papaya salad, and some dishes with fish, pork belly, duck, boar, and sticky rice. I loved that he was not intimidated by my appetite.

"So, tell me more about your childhood."

"I was hoping you had forgotten."

"I do not forget questions I've asked." This time it was my turn to laugh.

"Well, there's not much to tell. As I mentioned, my father left when I was born. Probably too scared to take on the responsibility. Who knows? My mother refused to talk about him. She tried the best she could while living with her parents, but I was a colic baby. At least that's what my new parents told me. When I was five months old, she put me up for adoption and luckily for me I got adopted by a nice suburban couple. They couldn't have kids and always treated me as one of their own, but they also weren't the really ambitious kind. Mom was a housewife and Dad was a lawyer. Dad was happy being at the bottom pushing papers around, and it made me mad the older I got. So I vowed that when I became a lawyer, I wouldn't do the same. And I think I've done a pretty good job of that."

"Well, that is quite a story. Did you ever see your birth mother again?"

"She tried once when I was twenty, but I never responded. Let's talk about something else."

"Okay, tell me a story that Sir Anthony has told you."

"What kind of story?"

"Any story. A story about him, about his house, about his life. Anything. I just want to learn more."

"I brought you out so you could get away from the house." He laughed out loud.

That surprised me. I loved his laugh. He had such a nice smile and straight white teeth. His face became more boyish instead of serious.

"Well, there's just so much to learn and who knows when I'll see you again. For all I know, if I don't extract more information from you every time I see you, stories that I would love to know will be lost."

"Wow, no need to be so dramatic," again with the laugh. It made me smile.

"Just tell me a story."

"Okay, let me think . . ." he was silent for a bit, but then sat up and looked me in the eyes.

"Holiday galas. Christmas was Sir Anthony's favorite time of year. And he always held a gala right around that time period. They got smaller over the years, but I think he still loved them."

"The holidays are my favorite time, too. Christmas especially. I just love the festiveness. I can't get enough of it."

"Well, you're in good company as Sir Anthony loved Christmas. He would start planning in August. Everyone in high society would start gossiping about who was on the invite-list. It was the social gathering of the season. I think that he didn't even care about who came. He just loved the holiday itself. He told me once he invited two enemies just for the fun of it, and that Christmas gala I believe is still talked about, but that's for another story. What he really liked were the decorations and the feeling of excitement and joy that came with Christmas. He loved standing in a corner and just looking out at all the festivities. There were garlands down the main staircase and every column. Lights were put up outside and inside the house—tastefully, not like the Griswold House. Huge wreaths were commissioned and he would add a new charm to the wreath each year. One wreath would go outside on the main door and another would go right over the main staircase. A Christmas tree would be put at the top of the staircase as well so that he would see it as soon as he walked out of his room and any guests arriving would see it as soon as they entered. He'd get the biggest one he could find, and you should have seen the piles of letters that arrived during that time begging him to buy their Christmas tree. Everyone would be in a festive mood in the household. It was like someone sprinkled pixie dust. There was a shine to everything and everyone had a hop in their walk and a smile on their face. Probably didn't hurt that he paid everyone double their wage for the last two weeks of December. He just loved everything about Christmas."

"Wow, that sounds amazing. I wish I could have seen one of those. How hard would it be to pull one off this year?" I asked.

"You want to put on a Christmas gala?"

"Yes, I would love to, and more importantly, I think it would really boost the staff's morale and let me get to know them a bit better."

"Have you ever planned anything like this before?"

"Not quite like this, but I have helped student organizations plan week-long events where a hundred people showed up, and I helped a past friend plan her wedding. I can do this."

"Well, if you think you can, I think the staff would help to make it happen. We could ask Andy when we get back to see what he thinks."

"We? Are you going to help me?"

"Why not," Sebastian chuckled. "I think it'll be fun to see how this goes. I might be able to give some input as I was with Sir Anthony when he planned the last few."

"I would definitely appreciate any help I can get, but I know you've got your lawyering to do."

"What are you saying? That I can't do two things at once?"

"Not at all." I laughed. "I just don't want you to feel obligated. I feel you've already gone beyond your call to duty checking on me."

"So, you're saying you've seen too much of me and I'm not welcome?"

"Not at all. Okay, let's start over. I would love to have your help," I said with much fanfare.

"It is my delight to help where I can," he said with equal fanfare. We both burst out laughing. There was something about Sebastian. I was comfortable around him.

Our food arrived, and the aroma made me start drooling. I knew we had ordered a lot, but seeing the dishes in person I was stunned.

"Bon appétit," he said.

"Bon appétit to you too. Good thing I didn't eat too much during the day."

We ate in silence for the next ten minutes. We were so ravenous.

"That was so delicious, but even I can't finish all of this food," I said through a mouthful.

"It's even better the next day," said Sebastian.

"Oh, I love leftovers."

"Me too. Everything gets nicely marinated," he said while looking up at me.

I laughed to myself as only I would go to dinner with someone and share a moment with him about leftovers.

"Why don't we go get those roses of yours? I know a great florist nearby. It's not a long walk."

"That would be great. I think you know everyone here."

"I did build up my business in this town. Had to start some-where," he shrugged.

When we left, there was a light dusting of snow. It was the perfect night, and I loved snow. I was out with a man I think I liked, and we got along great. Sebastian hooked my arm, and I gladly followed. We walked down the sidewalk a few blocks and ended up in front of the cutest boutique florist shop I had ever seen. The place could barely fit four or five people, and you felt like you were in a mini-garden walking around all the displays of flowers. Colors just everywhere framed by green foliage. And it smelled amazing. So fresh and clean.

"Sebastian! It has been too long! Who is this lady friend of yours?

Did I forget to send her some flowers for you?" she said winking at Sebastian. Clearly, subtlety was not her strong suit, but I liked her immediately. She had a full figure with a head of short, gray, curly hair. Her eyes were kind and twinkled behind thick-rim glasses. As she talked, her hands never stopped moving, pulling ribbons, wrapping flowers, rearranging, and cutting stems.

"Lucia, don't embarrass me," Sebastian said, laughing out loud. I loved that laugh. I would never get tired of it. "Anne is a client of mine, and she would like to get a dozen roses to bring home."

"Sebastian helped me with some legal matters when I opened this store five years ago. He is the best, and I only wish he wasn't so showy and expensive now."

"Lucia, I've told you time and time again that you should call me up whenever you need help. I will always help you."

"For a fee, though, yeah?"

"Well, of course, I have to make a living, too, but you'll get the family discount."

"Oh, Sebastian," she looked at him fondly, as if he was her own grandson.

"Those roses, Lucia?"

"A dozen roses coming up! You will love these. They have a hint of copper to them and shine. They just came in and are very fresh." She went to the back and rummaged around for a bit and came out with gorgeous, reddish-orange roses that shone when the light hit them. They would look great in my room.

"I love them. Do you take a credit card?"

"Lucia, just put them on my tab."

"No, Sebastian. You shouldn't buy flowers for me."

"Well, why not? This will be my housewarming gift to you since I know how much they mean to you."

"Thank you." I blushed.

"Sebastian—he has a good heart," Lucia said, looking fondly at us.

"Lucia, please just wrap it up," Sebastian said quickly, pulling me away from the counter.

Sebastian drove me home, gave me the tenderest kiss on the forehead, and said he'd see me tomorrow. I stood at the front door a bit longer looking at the car disappear down the driveway. Whatever tonight was I wouldn't have done anything differently. I didn't want to get my hopes up, but my heart swelled with the thought that I had hopefully found someone who was more than a friend. No one had ever treated me like he had.

19

KNOCK, knock, knock.

Please tell me that I imagined the knocking on my door. I hadn't slept very well and even though the sun was out, I was not ready to set my feet on the ground. But damn, the knocking was real.

"Who is it?" I groaned under my covers. Maybe they wouldn't hear me and would leave.

"It's Andy. I have your breakfast here for you." He must have ears of a wolf.

That was odd though. He had never brought me my breakfast before.

"Come in."

In came Andy, but what startled me was the young boy behind him.

"Good morning, Anne. I hope this is not too early, but it is already nine and I know you will be eager to meet the whole staff."

"The whole staff? Andy, who is this boy in my room?" I asked while pulling up the covers.

"Ah, yes, sorry. I should have warned you. Precisely why we need him. I am getting up in age if you didn't already notice, and Ben here is my replacement. He was hired almost a year ago by Sir Anthony and has been shadowing me."

"Ah, gotcha. Nice to meet you, Ben. The whole staff is home already?"

"Yes, that's why I've come. Cook wanted to make sure you were fed a proper breakfast before meeting everyone, and she knew you were still in bed, so she asked me to bring it up to you so you could take your time."

"That's awfully nice of her. It smells delicious as usual."

"I'll leave you be. There is no hurry. Come downstairs when you're ready."

"Thank you, Andy, and nice to meet you, Ben."

"It's nice to meet you as well, Ms. Anne."

"Anne is just fine." I laughed. "Oh, Andy, can I ask you something before you leave?"

"Of course."

"Would the staff be interested in helping me set up a Christmas gala like Sir Anthony used to have? Sebastian told me about them last night, and I thought it would be a great way to get everyone together and to get to know the staff better."

"Anne, that is a grand idea!" Andy beamed. "I will tell the staff immediately, and we will get started."

"Oh, I'd like to be part of the planning."

"You will be, do not worry, but some of the staff have gone through multiple galas. The mundane stuff we can get started on such as the decorations which will need to be taken out of storage and hung all over the house. It's tedious work, but everyone loves the feel and look when we're all done."

"That would be fantastic. I will help with everything." As soon as I said that, I remembered that I had only given myself a week off. Next week, I would have to start my blog posts up again and get back to meeting deadlines for articles. I would need to balance my job with the gala starting next week. It had only been four days, and I already didn't want to go back to reality. My Ai Po lived in this house. The thought still boggled my mind.

I uncovered the tray and started salivating. Buttery eggs and grits with a side of juicy bacon and some freshly made pancakes stared back at me while I snuggled deeper into bed. A tall glass of orange juice was the perfect complement for washing it all down. I could really get used to this.

After breakfast, I hopped out of bed eager to meet all the new staff. Eager and petrified. I knew everyone was already nervous about me, but I bet they didn't know I was equally nervous about getting their approval, too. I had never had help and had never even considered it. Did I need to make a speech? Oh, goodness.

At this point, I had unpacked all my items into my huge walk-in closet. All of my items fit in the first of four sections on one side. Even then, it still took me thirty minutes to narrow my choices down to three outfits. I decided to go semi-business. That would at least let me be comfortable while I shook and tried to talk intelligently in front of the crowd. Tentatively, I walked out onto the staircase and saw nobody. *Well, that was anticlimactic.*

"Hi Anne, I'll go get everyone if you'd like to meet them now?" said Ben coming out of nowhere. Where do these people hide?

"Yes, that would be good." It'll give me time to catch my breath. I wasn't sure where to stand, so I just sat down at the bottom of the stairs.

"A word of advice?"

"Yes?" I looked at him hopefully.

"You don't seem that mean so just be yourself. Andy and Cook have talked a lot about you and they've been here the longest so everyone looks up to them. They basically run the house."

"Thank you, Ben."

"You're welcome. I like you." He ran off before I could respond.

People started streaming in from all directions. And everyone wore suits or black dresses. That would be the first thing I would change. Color. Why are people so afraid of color? Most of them looked scared and looked at me as if I was this big shot staring down at them deciding their fate, which I realized was what I was. I saw

Andy and Cook and they both smiled at me, which put me a little at ease.

"Hi everyone, it's so good to meet you. My name is Anne Huang and I hope I get to know each and every one of you. I know many of you are nervous about having me here and are missing Sir Anthony. I have heard he was a genuine gentleman, and I only wish I had known him myself. I do not plan on changing anything in the household except for maybe the color of the uniform," I paused for laughter and none came "but um . . . I do plan on setting up the Christmas gala for this year. I think it will be a great tradition to help us get through this change."

"Are you going to pay us double like Sir Anthony did?" There were mumblings and groans from the crowd, and I heard "you shouldn't ask that right now," as well as "she seems nice," "will be nice to have a change around here," and "let's give her a chance," but it stung as I also heard "she's Chinese or some sort of Asian," "why would Sir Anthony give his fortune to someone outside of the family?" "you think the tales from his twenties are true?" "what does she know about American culture?" "geez, we're going to have to teach her everything," among other grumbles.

I was surprised because I expected everyone would be excited. A cough came from the back, and I looked to see Andy getting everyone's attention.

"We should let Anne continue." I stood up straighter and tried to look the part of a master while not feeling any inner strength at all.

"I plan on taking things slow. I know I'm new, but I love this house and all the history that has happened here. I want to preserve what's here, and yes, I do plan on paying all of you double just like Sir Anthony did. I . . ."

"Anne just learned about our gala yesterday. We should give her the same support we gave Sir Anthony. I agree the festivities will cheer all of us up and allow for something familiar for us to do this holiday season. Let's show her how we work together. I will take care of the guest list and Cook will, of course, create a fabulous meal for us. Daisy and Sandra, will you take a group to bring down the decorations from the attic? Let's aim to get those up first and see the house lit up again. I know Sir Anthony would want us to be festive this holiday season and not see us in mourning." I was appreciative of Andy interrupting me as I literally didn't know what else to say.

"I'll go check on the horses and the carriage," said one of the men.

"We have horses?" *Oops, did I just say that out loud?*

"Yes, they are usually in the stable behind the house, but since Sir Anthony's passing, they were moved to the vet's home who takes care of them. We weren't sure if you rode horses and thought they would have better care there, especially since the staff was not around," Andy said.

"Gotcha," I felt like a fool that I hadn't explored more of the house or asked more questions or just gotten to know the new home I was in. I had been so absorbed in my Ai Po's letters, but who wouldn't be right? At least that's what I told myself, but I could see some in the audience were surprised I didn't know I owned horses. Some in the audience just looked sorry for me.

"I'll help Cook dig out all the holiday china."

"We'll start airing out the spare bedrooms. You know how the Bocher family likes to take advantage of Sir Anthony's hospitality," someone said, and everyone laughed.

"You mean Anne's hospitality?" said Andy. Everyone went silent and looked at me only just remembering that I was still there. I hadn't felt like the new kid in class in a really long time. What I wouldn't do to have Victoria or Sebastian here right now.

"I don't want to change anything this year. Let's do everything as Sir Anthony had done before. I know we're getting a late start so if there is anything I can help with please let me know."

"Let's all go and do our tasks. Anne, why don't you come with me?" inquired Andy.

I was thankful for Andy's input and graceful way of exiting. I followed him into the sitting room and sat down among the pillows.

"I have no idea what I'm doing."

"You will get it. It'll just take time. Everything takes time."

"Is there anything I can help with now?"

"Not at the moment, but I will go and start the guest list. I'll show it to you when I am done, so you can look it over and add or delete anyone off of the list."

"That sounds great. I guess I'll go back to my room."

"Cook has set up a nice morning tea in the library for you. And the journals you and Sebastian were reading yesterday are still there. This is your home. Don't be a stranger."

"Thank you, Andy. That is more than generous of you and Cook. Please let the others know to come to me with anything."

I didn't know if I made a great impression this first time around, but Andy was right. This was my home, and I was not going to feel like a stranger in my own home. The library was set up just like Andy said, and I settled myself in front of the fire.

35年11月3日 (Sunday, November 3, 1946)

Anthony, as he wants me to call him, left for his Asia tour today. We spent the whole week doing conversational and business talk so that he sounded like he knew what he was talking about. His father joined in on one of the sessions and seemed to approve, but it left me petrified. His father scares me and always makes me feel like he has eyes everywhere. Father and son are so different from each other. But extra lessons were put in to get him as ready as possible. So much so that it was all I could do to remember to eat my meals. At least Marjorie would remind me to eat. She would always put a meal aside for me and send someone to get me to come to the kitchen if I didn't show up for meals. I would hit the pillow at the end of the night so hard I didn't even know I had laid down when I woke up the next morning. I will miss him. We spent everyday together much to the other staffs' ill looks. Andy and Cook have given up on chiding me, but they think Anthony is leading me on. With a father like Lord Anthony and a wishy-washy mom, no good can come out of the son. I don't believe a word they say as Anthony is the only one who treats me like a person. He's genuinely interested in my culture and my likes and dislikes. There is no judgment behind his questions. He's even embraced some new traits he's learned such as always putting his chopsticks flat on his plate and not jabbed into his bowl. I went to the bench a couple days ago, and he had left a note between the crack we found on the side of it. It was in rudimentary Chinese, but he had written it from top to bottom and even used a mao bi to paint the characters on. He had added plum blossoms to the corners of the note. My favorite flowers. In order to blend in, he asked me to make him a changshan for any formal events he had to go to. It was my privilege to make something beautiful for him. In addition, I tailored a couple suits for him as he had lost weight during the war. I'm falling for him so badly, and I'm trying hard to fight it even though it doesn't look like it to others. He's so nice and caring and I love his laugh. He treats me well even though he doesn't have to. It's nice to not be a sideline object to someone else's life but to actually be noticed. Is there anything wrong with wanting that? He won't be here for a month so I have time to get over him. Lady Mary has requested more dresses to be made for her. What she does with her old ones I have no idea, but all I can think is that I could re-purpose them for others to wear if she's just going to hang them and let them collect dust. I hope I'm never so rich that I start wasting everything. Maybe one day I'll suggest that to her. She's definitely not as scary as Lord Anthony. But who knows, maybe she's one of those quiet evil types. Anthony has three sisters and a brother. Jack has been very nice to me as well and is the same age as me, but he keeps to himself and writes, draws, or plays the piano. I'm not really sure what he does. Bernice worked during the war fixing airplane engines, and I can hear her and her mom fighting all the time about how she doesn't want to marry whoever her mom wants to set her up with. She wants to get a job continuing her work on engines. At least this is what Andy and Marjorie tell me. Catherine is radiant. She wears the brightest clothes she can get her hands on, which is slowly becoming more available, but a lot of them I'm making for her. She's fourteen and already talking about this boy, Thomas, she wants to marry. Her mother ignores her, but I can tell this girl has a mind of her own as well. If no one notices she's going to get married, then there will be nothing anyone can do about it. The youngest, Geraldine, is ten, and she's the prettiest one of them all. Her mom curls her hair into tight bouncy locks, and she's always in a cute dress with some ruffles on the bottom. She copies her dad and pretends to be stern with me. I notice her hiding behind doors and corners staring at me. She'll call me something mean and then run off laughing. Anthony has been there a couple of times and will run after her, chiding her, but there is such a big age difference, and he does love her so that I think it ends up being more of a tickle war than an actual lecture. Since I've been here, I've been called every name possible. At least it sure seems like it. Chinawoman, Chink, Yellow woman, an Oriental, a no-good, job stealer, brown noser, and I can't remember the others. I'm quite used to being treated as a low-class person as I'm a girl and my family was not that well-to-do but to stand out so much because of the way I look stings. Good thing I have a mule personality, though my mom says it's more a detriment than a good thing. Having Anthony hang out with me all the time makes me forget all the nasty comments. Plus, Andy and Marjorie are my friends, and they are starting to prove themselves very well, and the family and staff love them. Sometimes, it's just you and me, journal. Marjorie wants me to teach her some of the food and baked goods I can make, and in return, she'll teach me her recipes. I'm very excited about this!

35年11月6日 (Wednesday, November 6, 1946)

Cook was wonderful and let me stay by her side through the whole lunch process. I had no idea one could use so much cream in a soup, but wow, did it taste good. She also taught me how to make a carrot cake. I have nicks on my finger from grating the carrots, but it beat using only a knife to slice into tiny pieces. The walnuts were chopped until I could fit one right on the tip of my pinkie. The cake came out airy and moist with the perfect amount of carrot and walnuts dispersed all throughout. The cream cheese icing was like nothing I had before. I want more! I like it better than buttermilk icing. Not as sweet. I love cheese even though my stomach doesn't. I cannot get enough of the richness of the American foods. They are decadent and delicious. Andy showed me around to some other parts of the house, but my favorite is still the garden. Being out in nature and not having to walk very far at all and to have it quiet and peaceful. I wish to have a garden of my own in the future. Maybe Aunt Ruby has a garden, and one day I could move down to be with my family. Mom and Dad like getting my letters and they say they're doing well. Business is good, and maybe, in a couple of years, I can move in with them. I got my first check as well, and they were happy to receive it as it equaled both of theirs put together. I didn't tell them about Sir Anthony. They would never approve of me being this close to a boy even if it's just for tutoring purposes. And a boy who was not Chinese. I might as well never marry.

35年11月11日 (Monday, November 11, 1946)

Cook has taught me Italian, French, Mexican, and I, in turn, taught her some Chinese dishes. My favorite, of course, fried rice. It's so simple, but the right amount of oil and the right ingredients at the right time, and it makes all the difference. Everything has to be chopped super fine and Cook was not used to that. All her meats were slabs of at least one centimeter thick. I can't wait to learn more. I heard Lady Mary talking about a Christmas gala. I think I heard that right. I have no idea what a Christmas or a gala is, but maybe these dresses are for that. She has taken such a big interest in these particular dresses. She visits me every day to check on my progress. I do have to say that the detailing on this dress is going to take me weeks, but it's going to look ravishing. Her daughter's dresses are more muted, maybe to allow the mother to shine, but they're still going to be ravishing in their own right. Where she got all this lace is beyond me, but it's definitely giving me a challenge.

35年11月18日 (Monday, November 18, 1946)

I got a letter from Anthony! It was addressed to my Chinese name, and I thought it was from my parents, but it was from Anthony! He must have gotten a native to write on the envelope as the inside was where he had written in his rudimentary Chinese interspersed with English. It was short and just said hello and hoped I was doing well and that he had been thinking of me. He now understood why I hated the sea and why I never wanted to get on a boat again. He was thinking of me. I cannot get over that. I'm glad I was in my room when I opened the letter. I nearly fainted. If anyone else had seen this letter, I don't know what I would have done. Probably just stood there gob-struck like I was currently doing in the safety of my room.

35年11月20日 (Wednesday, November 20, 1946)

I've decided I'm going to write back to him. I'll sneak the letter in the pile by the door so no one will ever know. Andy has taken up my English tutoring. He and Anthony seemed to have a pretty good relationship, and I saw Anthony talking to him before he left and pointing in my direction. I like Andy. He's trustworthy and is really good at his job. I'll put in some new words I've learned into the letter, but maybe I should keep this one short as his first one was short. I definitely talk too much, but I really want to share everything that has been going on with him.

Later the same day . . . I decided to keep it short and mentioned I was making a new creation of dresses for his mom and sister, helping with the gala, and I even wrote some of it in English to show how much I had learned. There was already a big pile of mail by the door, so, win for me! Great, now I'm going to be a nervous wreck because I don't know if he'll get the letter or if he'll send one back.

35年11月23日 (Saturday, November 23, 1946)

Andy and Cook have both told me I'm really antsy these days. I can't tell them about the letter as they would not talk to me anymore. They already disapproved of me spending so much time with Anthony. I'm so nervous. Will he actually write back? I need to find something else to focus on. I've asked Andy to tutor me every day and to add more American customs. So we do an hour a day when we both have breaks. Lady Mary's dress is coming along nicely and she is happy with it. All the bead and lace work needs to be started this week.

35年11月26日 (Tuesday, November 26, 1946)

I'm so crumpled up inside and have no one to share it with. The collar of Lady Mary's dress is almost done. She wanted some lacework done. I've never done so much lacework, but I wasn't going to say no to her. That would be the end of my work here. Betsy was really nice and showed me some tips she had learned from her Ai Po. Luckily, my years of garment making allowed me to learn fast. Betsy said I have talent, but I just hope Lady Mary doesn't notice all the flaws.

35年11月29日 (Friday, November 29, 1946)

Aaaahhhhh!!!!! Started on the bodice. Hand sewing all these little beads is driving me crazy, and I still have the rest of the dress to do! If anything, it's helping me keep my mind off of Anthony.

35年12月2日 (Monday, December 2, 1946)

If I could pull out my hair, I would. But the thought of Lord Anthony questioning me is keeping me from doing it. He scares me to no end. Bodice work, bodice work . . . how I hate the bodice work . . . I have been working on these dresses non-stop as Lady Mary has given me two more designs to start working on which she wants to be done for New Year's. When I first moved here, I wondered why the family needed me. I'm sure there were seamstresses around who could do the work I was doing. I have since learned I get paid a lot less than anyone here, even the stable boy. She also gives me so many outfits to make, alter, or fix that it's a full-time job just for this household. She gets these ideas from her friends and comes to me asking if I can make it happen as soon as possible. What am I supposed to say? No? I fall asleep like a log most nights with no time to write. On a happy note, I now know what Christmas and a Gala is and it's all due to Andy's hard work on teaching me English. He found a children's book about Christmas in the library for me to read. The pictures were my favorite, especially all the red in the book as it reminded me of all the red used in our tradition. It's so festive and happy. Makes me want to smile every day. At least something is making me happy. He makes me respond to him in as much English as I can, and he has asked me to answer the other staff members in English as much as I can. The longer I stay, and the harder I work, I've noticed a few starting to want to learn Chinese, too. It's been fun sharing languages and culture with them. Lord Anthony, on the other hand, I think just dislikes people who aren't rich, aren't white, and aren't like him. I've never seen him laugh or smile amongst any of the staff members. I feel like a fool for writing a letter back to Sir Anthony. I have received nothing back. It takes a long time, I know, but how can I show my face to him when he comes back. He must think me a silly girl for thinking someone like me could think of him, the master of the house, as someone I could even like. But that's enough moping. I know you want to hear more about what's exciting in my life. Thank you for listening, though. Cook or Andy would never understand. They're so dedicated to their jobs. I dream of one day owning a place of my own and being the master. One can dream, can't they? I'll show them. I saw delivery trucks bringing in greenery shaped in circles and long strands maybe five meters long. On them were brown, spiky, triangular shaped objects, which Andy told me were pine cones, as well as a beautiful, bright red bow that finished off the look. They were all piled up by the entrance, and Betsy said that they were going to start decorating the house tomorrow, and I can't wait to see how it turns out. I was going to help them hang everything. She said there were a lot of beautiful glass trees and bright colored nutcrackers they were going to bring down from the attic as well. These objects had been collected over the years and there was quite an assortment to spread throughout the house. I'm not sure why anyone would want a nut-breaking kitchen tool decorating their house, but all these new findings fascinate me. She also said that the family had decided on who to get their tree from this year, and it was supposed to be grander than the year before. From the book, I read it looked like they decorated it with objects and lights. I didn't understand it all, but I was excited nonetheless.

My eyes were getting bleary, but I had to tear myself away from Ai Po's journals. I so wanted to know what happened and I couldn't believe the things I was reading. I wondered how much my mother knew about these events and maybe this was why she never talked about Ai Po. But then again these journals were newly found. A headache was also starting from concentrating so much. Plus, I was getting hungry. I didn't want to admit it, but I probably needed a break. They were all-encompassing and if this morning's speech had told me anything I needed to get to know my house and the staff a bit better if I was really going to be living here.

I ventured into the kitchen, and the smell of beef stew wafted up. It was noisier than ever and there were more people in the kitchen now. Cook was running around with sweat rolling down her face. She saw me and yelled something, but I couldn't hear her. She came rumbling over and met me halfway.

"You should not be in here today. The whole staff is home, and I have a lot of cooking to do. I already put your meal aside and told Lavender to bring it up to you. Cripes 'ol mighty! The stupid girl didn't take it. Lavender!"

"It's quite all right. I can take it myself."

"No, that is not the proper way. You are the master now and you should act as such. Let us do our jobs. Lavender is lazy and someone needs to put her in line. Please go back upstairs and she will bring the food up to you."

"I—"

"Go. She will bring the food up to you."

I left feeling awful while Cook screamed Lavender's name over and over. As I was leaving the kitchen, I saw a small head pop up from the back of the kitchen. She seemed like she had fallen asleep. I felt so bad for her, but Cook seemed overstressed as well. Waiting in the library, I took the time to look around at the books that were actually on the shelf. Mathematics, physics, history, novels that were so old the lettering on the spine was barely readable, to modern novels by Michael Crichton, medical books detailing every aspect of the body, and biology books talking about ferns, lions, rodents, and sea life. You name it, if you wanted to research a certain topic this library probably could get you started on, if not completely through your research. I had climbed the ladder to reach more books on higher shelves when I heard hard breathing and the clattering of silverware. Lavender came in with cheeks red, sweat running down her face, and eyesight down not daring to look at me. She probably got a good reprimanding from Cook. I clambered down the ladder and went to meet her before she ran off.

"I'm so sorry, Ma'am, for not bringing up your food. I haven't been sleeping well, and I fell asleep at the back of the kitchen before the food was completely done, and I'm *so* sorry."

"Lavender, it's really okay. I'm glad you didn't bring up the food earlier as I was too engrossed in these journals. This way I was able to stop reading when I wanted to."

"Oh, well it might have been good for me to come up earlier anyway so you wouldn't read too much." I watched as her eyes got big, and her hand went to her mouth.

"Why would you say that?"

"I can't stop myself. Cook says I have some sort of disease that keeps my mouth from closing before my thoughts come out."

"Lavender, really though, why would you say that?"

"It's nothing. Please don't pay me no mind. I only heard Cook and Andy talking and Cook was mad at Andy for not making those journals disappear. I really didn't hear anything else. I should go now."

Lavender walked away, but with her head held low and her feet dragging reluctantly to head back to her station. Why would Cook not be happy with me reading Ai Po's journals? I knew better than to head to the kitchen to ask and the beef stew was calling. But the question kept circling in my mind.

20

THE BEEF STEW calmed my nerves, and I decided that for today I would go and explore the house instead of reading more even though I was itching to. I started walking toward the gardens when I bumped into Andy.

"Anne, could I see you for a minute. I want to go over the guest list."

"Of course, but I'm not sure I will recognize anyone on the list." We went to his office, and I saw a tome sitting on his desk.

"I would like you to take this list and study it." He walked around his desk.

"Study it?" I looked at the book, suddenly petrified. I didn't even study travel books in detail.

"I'd like you to memorize as many of the names as you can and let me know if you'd like to add anyone else to the list. Thankfully, the invitations will be going out late this year so there will probably not be as many people who come, but it's best to be ready," Andy said as he handed me a ten-page, twelve-point-font list of hundreds of names, where they were from, what companies they ran, and what relations they were to Sir Anthony.

"This is daunting but I can do it," I barely breathed out. "I thought you wanted me to go over that big book on your desk," I laughed.

"I was, but many of these are deceased or aren't invited this year. I took the liberty to comb over the initial list already. I hope that was okay," he said in all seriousness.

"No, that's fine," thinking, *how does someone know so many people? And thank goodness I don't have to memorize the book.* I glanced through the hundreds of names, dazzled by the Lords and Ladies, but also by all the names of aunts, uncles, cousins, nieces, nephews, grand-nieces and nephews, and grand-grand nieces and nephews. Would the whole family really be coming to the gala? I suddenly started wondering if this was such a good idea. It seemed there were people from all over the world. I looked up at Andy and must have had a petrified look on my face. I surely felt like I had frozen and couldn't move.

"Do not worry. No one expects you to remember every single person on this list. I just want you to remember as many as you can. It might make you feel more at ease to know who could come and what they do."

"Yes, I agree. There's . . . just . . . so . . . many . . ."

"The gala will not be for another month so you have time. Let me know who you want to add today. I'll have Ben go into town tomorrow to get the invitations ordered and sent out. We'll rush them so they go out by this weekend. Also, when you can tomorrow, sit down with Cook to go over the menu. She has done it for so long she has a pretty set one that accounts for allergies, food dislikes, and foods that everyone just expects her to make, but I know she'll want to make some of your favorites. And the staff is going to start decorating today, so they'll need to meet with you to see how much you want to cover the house in Christmas garlands etc. and—"

"Andy, thank you so much. I don't know what I'd do without you. All of those sound great. I will go find Cook after this and grab a snack while I'm there, and I'll walk around with you later today to see the decorations."

I grabbed my coat, headed out the front door, and plopped myself on the front deck. The path I drove in on stretched as far as the eye could see and I wondered for the millionth time what had happened to my life. I was disappointed that Sebastian hadn't stopped by today. He was my sounding board, and I missed having his presence, but it was a Tuesday, wasn't it? Most people didn't have the luxury to take a week off and have the ability to consider not going back. Would I really ever consider that? I looked down at the guest list in my hands and sighed. I better get started on this and not be the cog that held everyone back.

I went back to the library, bundled myself in front of the fire, and spent the next few hours pouring over the list. How was I supposed to remember these names? Mr. and Mrs. Victorkamang whose family owned one of the biggest breweries in Europe, Cynthia Chu whose family owned a big jewelry company I had never heard of (but that's not saying much as I wore no jewelry). There were people from the Tech Sector—computers, chips, lighting, space, and all their significant others including kids, and in some cases, cousins, aunts, and uncles. And then, of course, there was the long list of family members. A few of the names I recognized. It would be really nice to see Jack again. I wouldn't mind if he was the only member of the family to come, but I couldn't be picky. This was my first gala after all. Andy was sitting at his desk when I returned.

"Andy, I'm only going to add my mom, Victoria, and Sebastian to the list. Did you want to go look at the decorations?"

"Great, I will have Ben go now and get the invitations sent. Yes, let's go look at decorations."

I wasn't sure why they needed my opinion, but Andy led me to the very end of the third floor. There was a staircase that led up to the attic.

"Follow me and mind your step. The attic is very old, and the Wilkens never threw anything out."

I followed Andy and stopped in my tracks at the top of the floor. It was a very well-lit room with lots of people bustling around. Right in front of me were trunks stacked to the ceiling. They could have held blankets, memorabilia like what I found in Ai Po's chest, or they could have held what literally covered the ground and walls of half of the attic. There were five people up here. Some were digging through trunks, some stacking boxes of ornaments on the side, some unwinding Christmas lights, some cussing up a storm because they couldn't get to where they needed to be, and some sorting the prettiest nutcrackers, glass Christmas trees, garlands, and wreaths I had ever seen. There were different sizes of everything and literally enough stuff to cover the house. It was my very own Christmas store! I immediately smiled and felt all my energy coming back to me.

"We have to use all of this decoration."

"Well, that does answer one of my questions. Do you only want to do the places where people will see? Front of the house, foyer, library, sitting room, ballroom? Or do you want to do more, such as the stables and back of the house?"

"All of it. Whatever you guys used to do."

"Well, we used to do the whole house when Sir Anthony was younger, but as he aged we narrowed down the spaces. It's really up to you how much we should do. As you can see, some of the items being pulled out have broken or are so tangled we're not sure if we can untangle them."

"Let's do all the big areas you mentioned and see what kind of supply we have left. I can help. I love decorating for Christmas and there are so many pretty objects here to really make the place look festive. Where can I start?" I looked at everyone expectantly.

They had stopped working while I was talking and were just looking at me. I felt very self-conscious and wasn't sure what to do, but I looked at Andy who gave me a nod and I went forward and started unraveling one of the Christmas tree lights. I loved Christmas and damn if anyone was going to put me in a sour mood about it.

21

FOR THE REST of the week, I helped decorate the house. The house seemed to quadruple in size and the decorations were never-ending. Sebastian wasn't able to visit the rest of the week, and I was disappointed, but he managed to send me roses every day. I had spread them all over the house so I could think of him every time I walked by one. For some reason, he hadn't sent back his RSVP for the gala, and I really missed someone to talk to. I had started looking forward to him showing up unannounced and sharing what I was learning here with him. *Tomorrow*, I told myself, *I have to do some work.* I had placed sticky notes all over my room to remind me of the many things I needed to accomplish. Each day of the week had its own sticky note color. Sticky notes even made it into the library on books about Australia, New Zealand, Taiwan, China, Japan, and Korea. I was walking in and out of my room thinking that I was forgetting something when I saw Andy walk up the stairs.

"Why don't you take today off," said Andy.

I blew out a deep breath, "I might take you up on that offer. I'm really stressed and not thinking straight."

"If I may point out the obvious. You inherited billions of dollars and a house. You found your grandmother's journals. You are learning the history of your family, and if I remember right, you have articles to submit that you haven't started on."

"Yeah, that about sums it up. I think I'll go see my mom for a couple of days."

"Take your time. We're not going anywhere." I thought I might have seen the first sign of a small smile appear, but it disappeared as fast as it came.

Mom was so excited when I told her I was going to come back and stay with her for a couple days. She started planning out our days together. I had to burst her bubble to let her know I had work to do and probably couldn't go out too much, but lunch would be great and I couldn't wait to eat her cooking.

Victoria, I left a message letting her know about the gala in case the invitation never got to her. I really hoped she could make it. Sebastian also received a message from me letting him know I would be out of town for a couple of days. I missed him, and if he wanted to come up to Astoria, I would love to show him around.

"Andy, do you think I belong here?"

"Of course, Sir Anthony did not think lightly on this topic."

"I know it's probably something to do with my Grandmother, but why? Even if they had a thing for each other, it doesn't mean someone would give their fortune to a non-family member, especially since he had family members he liked."

"I cannot tell you exactly why, but I think you should keep reading."

"Cook doesn't think I should have read those journals."

"Cook has her opinions, and they are valid for her, but I think you will understand once you finish reading."

"Okay, Andy. I won't pry more."

"By the way, you can take more than two days at home if you want to spend more time with your mother. The staff has seen how hard you work, and I have heard some say how appreciative they are that you are willing to get your hands dirty."

"Oh, it just feels wrong to leave since I'm the one who wanted this gala."

"It's okay to rely on us. That's what you pay us for after all."

"Right, need to remember that part. Well, I think I'll go take a walk through the garden some more and look for some more of the children-statues."

"Ah, yes . . ." said Andy. It looked like his eyes glazed over and he was in a far-off memory.

"I found a bench in a private spot where there's a little boy on a blanket. Sebastian said there are others of the boy at different ages. I wanted to go see if I could find them."

I thought I had lost him when he whispered, "There are those around the house as well."

"Andy, what is the story behind these statues?"

"That is for another day," he susurrated, awakening from his dream. "I must get back to the others to make sure everything is still moving forward. I will let the driver know that you wish to leave after lunch. I will be in touch if there's anything you need, but take your time," and with that, he got up and left.

What was up with people not answering my questions? Cook had also stayed tight-mouthed since that one time when I asked her about Ai Po. In any case, I was excited to go explore. I went and said hi to the little boy who I started calling Billy. Then I walked back out of the spiral and away from the house to explore deeper into the garden. A low hedge about three feet tall lined the path on my right-side. Every 50 feet or so was a 20-foot tree. The whole path was lined with them. I followed the path until I saw an opening on my left. This one had the same tree, but it was a little taller than the rest. All the trees looked like they were budding. I couldn't wait to see what kind of flowers came out. Under the tree was a circular bench that wrapped around the base of the tree. On the other side of the tree I saw another opening, and through that door, I saw two more paths that went off to different rooms of the garden. It looked like Lord and Sir Anthony had designed the garden to be its own mansion with separate bedrooms. I found three statues in various rooms while walking around for the next few hours. One looked like a five-year-old reaching up into a tree to grab at something in the branches. Another looked like a ten-year-old walking down the path while brushing his finger along the hedge, head tilted as if deep in his own thoughts. The last one I found was a woman sitting under a tree in a calf-length dress, a belt around her waist, her hair braided and resting across the front of her shoulder, reading a book. The detail and thought put into all the statues was amazing. I wondered if Sir Anthony brought the kids from the Children's Hospital to visit and enjoy his garden. It would make anyone feel relaxed and happy. As the sun set, I turned to look back at the house and someone had turned on the Christmas lights that were finished. We were able to salvage a lot and the back of the house lit up every roofline, window, and the deck shone like a boat out at sea, beckoning for someone to bring it home. I loved it.

22

THE NEXT WEEK WAS A BLUR. My mother was glad to see me and never asked me about Ai Po's journals. She would change the topic whenever I brought it up. I ended up staying through Sunday, and by then, I was drained and wished I was back at the house. All my work got turned in, but it was hard to walk around town because I was a mini-celebrity. The attention was nerve-racking, but I refused to let anyone make me feel that I couldn't come back home, so I visited the places I would usually go to, such as Market Café. Ai Po's journal was always on me, but I hadn't gotten a chance to read it.

"Long time no see. Where is Miss Victoria?" said Adrian who had served us since we started coming years ago.

"She is exploring Europe trying to find herself."

He chuckled and shook his head. "Would you like your usual?"

"Yes, I would." I looked around at all the people sitting and walking by with some of them turning to do a double-take at me. I should have covered myself up better but there was nothing I could do about it now. Basking in the feeling of familiarity, I pulled out Ai Po's journal and rubbed my hand across the surface. My heart ached to share this with my mother, but she kept closing me off. Why wouldn't she want to know about her own mother's life?

35年12月6日 (Friday, December 6, 1946)

Today I took a break. Lord and Lady Wilkens and all the kids are out of the house and many of the staff are out doing errands, so everyone else is feeling a bit lazy. I didn't care if anyone yelled at me. I was working so much that my hands were cramping and bleeding from all the beadwork. My eyes get disoriented when I focus for too long. But the dresses are half way through and look exquisite. Lady Wilkens and her daughters love the dresses and can't wait to show them off to everyone they know. I've heard them telling their friends about it over tea. It secretly makes me proud inside. These outfits are my masterpieces. I've even been able to explain some of my work to them in English. I'm not sure if I'm saying everything correctly, but they nod and genuinely look happy. All thanks to Andy. He has been a great tutor, and we're able to have more conversations in words instead of hand gestures. It is liberating to be able to communicate again with just words. I must remember this for when I have kids someday. Words are the most important skill to have. Today, I am going to visit Cook and learn more about cooking. She is the one person who never wanted a break. She also tells me the most fascinating stories about her family and where she got some of her recipes. I don't think she is capable of staying quiet for very long. She is teaching me how to season American food and in turn, I am teaching her more Chinese cuisine. She is soaking up everything like a sponge. She has even mastered slicing meat into teeny-tiny bite-size pieces and marinating them even better than I can. It's amazing to watch her in action. She's as good at cooking as I am at sewing. We both love to create.

35年12月7日 (Saturday, December 7, 1946)

I forgot to mention the Christmas decorations yesterday. It's beyond anything I could have imagined, and I have a pretty good imagination. It's like we transformed the whole house into a winter castle, and I am officially living in a fantasy land of my very own. Everywhere I look everything is covered in white, red, or green. Gold ribbons line columns, doorways, and hallways. Every entrance to any room is decorated in some way or fashion. The wreaths were hung on all the outside doors with candles in every window, and every candle was covered in a glass cover. Thank goodness. I always thought it crazy my neighbors lit firecrackers right by their houses, but an open fire in every window takes a close second. It's still early, but I so wish to get a letter from Anthony. He should have left Asia by now and is hopefully making his way home. I wonder how his trip is and if we'll continue his Chinese lessons when he gets back. I wonder what he thought of my letter. I'm such a silly girl to think that someone like him would have any interest in me. I don't know what I'm thinking, but he makes my heart flutter and I can't stop thinking of him. Andy and Cook say I'm very distracted and think that I'm overworking as I spend quite a lot of time on these dresses. I'm so proud of my creations, and it's very sweet of them to worry about me, but if they only knew what was really on my mind.

I hate to admit I skimmed through a lot of the next week as she was downtrodden from not hearing back from Sir Anthony even though she knew perfectly well that it would take a while for him or a letter to get to her.

35年12月14日 (Saturday, December 14, 1946)

This whole week has been hustle and bustle and every able body was asked to help with getting the house ready for the party in less than two weeks. Who knew there could be so much to do to throw a party for your friends? Every piece of china and utensil had to be polished and there was A LOT. The Christmas tree finally got fully decorated. But I diverge from why I'm writing today. I really want to believe it, I don't want to get my hopes up, but it couldn't be from anyone else. I received a package today addressed to me in Chinese in a different handwriting. Inside was a red silk qipao with gold plum blossoms on them. It was beautiful and perfect for the Christmas gala coming up. Exactly my taste. Though I didn't know if I still had to wear my black uniform the day of the gala. There was a note written in Chinese that only said "I hope you enjoy it. I know how much you have missed home." It looked like it was not sent in America, but then one of my relatives could have sent it knowing how much I like new dresses. I had told my parents how much I missed home and how I wished we could move back and just go back to the way things were. That was a while ago, but maybe they asked my aunt to send me something. Maybe he sent it to me as a present and didn't include anything about him in case someone found out. One can wish, right? I don't know how I'm going to concentrate until he gets home. I just looked at my work table and I know how I'm going to stay busy. Lord Anthony has added to the pile and wants a couple of new suits made, so I'm tailoring a lot of his shirts because he has lost weight even though I never thought he had any fat to lose.

35年12月20日 (Friday, December 20, 1946)

I finished the dresses! Thank goodness. Lady Mary and the girls have been making changes every single day this week. They want the hem shorter, then they want it slightly longer, then the beadwork on the right side is just that much more than the left side, the lacework needs to be added here and here, and on and on. It was a good thing Andy kept bringing me food to eat, and that I managed to sneak in ten-minute naps here and there. My hands have ached so much throughout the week that I don't know if they will recover. I do have to say the dresses look absolutely stunning. I even added some red and green buttons along the spine of their dresses. They will shine as hostesses. Lord Anthony's shirts and suits are done as well. Now I just need to press all of them. As if everyone doesn't already have enough to do we were told yesterday that all staff is on hand to get the house shining clean for Sir Anthony's arrival on Sunday as well as all the family that will be coming in town and staying here with us. My heart pounds with the thought that I will see him soon. Thank goodness no one here can read my journals. Will he even acknowledge me?

35年12月22日 (Sunday, December 22, 1946)

I woke to people running down the hallway toward the front door. It was like a stampede of animals rushing to their next feed. When I got there, I had to jump behind all the people that were pushed against the window. Slowly, the sea opened, and I saw Anthony climb out of an everyday car. He looked more handsome than I remembered, and he had gotten some sun, which, thank goodness, helped him look less pasty. I couldn't take my eyes off of him, and I think he saw me, too, because he glanced my way and smiled, but he quickly looked away. My heart was thumping so hard I'm surprised no one else was looking at me.

A while later everyone was pushing past me and there was a line of people waiting to get into the car to look at something. None of the Wilkens asked any of the staff to move either. I didn't dare get too close to Anthony, so I looked on from the front stairs. It seemed that there was something large in the person's hand while sitting in the passenger seat. Then I heard people talking about a phone. What would a phone be doing in a car? While the others kept drooling over this phone thing, I looked back at Anthony. His siblings were giving him hugs and how I wished I could have greeted him in a similar fashion. I couldn't stay for long since there were details on the outfits for the Christmas gala that I still had to do. Lady Mary had bragged about my work so much that some of her relatives that were coming had sent their dresses ahead to have me add or fix certain things. Lady Mary had even hired an extra seamstress for the week to help me get through all the work. She was good, but I wish I could have done everything myself. I know, I have too high of a standard, but these are my creations. We worked all day, and just now, before I picked you up to write, I found a note tucked under my pillow with a picture of a plum blossom tree with a bench under it. He wanted to see me. I don't know if I can hold myself together until tomorrow!

35年12月23日 (Monday, December 23, 1946)

There is so much to tell you. I skipped breakfast and went straight to the bench. He hadn't put a time down and I couldn't sleep all night. I was only semi-surprised when I didn't see him there. On the bench was a pink plum blossom flower. It looked like it had been dried between the pages of a book. There were no footprints anywhere, and I wondered when it was set there. I picked it up and noticed in the gap under the flower there was something sticking out. Out came a note addressed to me, in Chinese! This time the Chinese was written in a childlike handwriting as if the person had just learned Chinese and was writing in big block letters minding every single stroke he was making. I smiled inwardly and could feel my whole face glowing. Tearing the note open, I saw the familiar pink plum blossoms drawn in the corner. The letter was a mix of Chinese and English—and I could tell his Chinese was improving.

Here, Ai Po had taped the note. Seeing the note in person really gave me a new perspective. It was one thing to be reading Ai Po's story just from her perspective, but to see actual writing from someone else during her lifetime during the same story somehow made it more real. I would have thought Andy and Cook being mentioned would have made it real, but neither one would share any information with me, so I guess I never really connected them.

Dear Rose,

Receiving your letter was the happiest day of my trip. I am learning new customs, especially how to work with the Oriental people. It never occurred to me how different they are in their customs and everyday life. I find it refreshing and especially like the love of family everyone focuses on. I wish you were here to guide me, and maybe next time you can travel with me as my translator and guide. But the hospitality has been fantastic. Business is going well, too. I was able to make it to Taiwan, and I loved it. One day, I hope to bring you home to visit with you. I cannot wait to share all my experiences with you and to get your feedback on certain matters. I hope you enjoyed the dress I sent. I had it made just for you. The flowers reminded me of you and I could not help myself but get it. I want to see you, but we must be careful, as you well know. My Chinese lessons will continue with you and we can find a warmer spot to do them, such as the library. I will continue writing notes and will leave them here in the bench. We could use this as our secret message place. I have missed you and hope you are doing well.

    Sincerely,

    Anthony

I was glowing from head to toe—I couldn't be happier. It made me extra happy that I had played a role in helping him with this trip. I will cherish this letter forever. I had no time to dwell on it as tomorrow is the gala and I told Cook I would help with some entrees. In light of Anthony's return from Asia, she wanted to make some of my mother's Chinese dishes to celebrate the successful trip. Luckily, the dresses and tux were all done, and no one has requested more changes. I'm crossing my fingers. I'm hoping I'll be able to see him tomorrow. I'm so extremely happy right now.

35年12月24日 (Tuesday, December 24, 1946)

    I felt like a fairy fluttering around the rooms dazzled by the imagery in front of me. All the best-dressed men and women in such foreign looking outfits. Ideas kept pouring into my mind, and I couldn't wait to try out some new dresses. There were diamonds, pearls, rubies, and gems I had never seen before. Cook outdid herself and she mastered the Chinese cuisine like a pro. I ate in the kitchen, of course, but she left a good size helping for all the staff. We had our own feast and merriment. People were dancing on the tables and I felt included for the first time. We would take turns going up to help with food or whatever was needed so we could see what was going on. There were so many people. I saw Anthony a few times, and every time the same girl was talking to him, putting her hands on his arm, laughing with him, and making me jealous. I don't like the feeling, but he washed it all away when he kissed me. Journal, he kissed me! I didn't want to tell you too soon in this entry because then I would never write about the gala, but I've never been kissed before. His lips were so tender and his skin smooth against mine sending a shiver all the way down to my toes. I still feel it just thinking about it. He found me in the hallway coming back from helping Cook in the kitchen and led me to the library. He was showing me some of his favorite novels and some that he had brought back from Asia. Then he just leaned over and kissed me. We looked at each other for a split-second and then he went back to showing me his books, but I could see a slight smile that wasn't there before. I'm sure I had one, too. We are supposed to start up lessons tomorrow and I can't wait. I don't know if I'll be able to sleep tonight. Don't worry if you don't hear from me soon. I really have to do well at these lessons. I want to keep seeing him.

I was so engrossed I didn't even know it was the end of the journal until I tried turning the last page and there were none. Their first kiss. There had to be more! This was my very own soap opera, and it was my own Ai Po! I had gone through three cups of coffee without even knowing it and eaten enough croissants to keep me from being hungry for dinner. My mom was not happy that I was so invested in these journals, but this was more information about my own family than I had ever heard before.

Andy had been calling me every day this week to go over details for the gala: seating arrangements, colors of the lights on the Christmas trees because there was more than one, the layout of the ballroom to coerce the group to mingle in certain areas, eat in certain areas, and dance in certain areas. This wasn't even including the politics of the family and friends that were coming. Andy was quizzing me on all the names and relationships just as he said he would, but I had no idea so many people could hate or love each other so much. It was its own soap opera, and I was already reading of another one.

Andy also mentioned there were more people coming this year than in the last ten years. Apparently, whole families were changing their plans to come because they were curious about meeting me. I cried myself to sleep that night once again wondering why I had taken this on in the first place. Andy kept saying he didn't need me there, but it just felt wrong to not be there when I was the hostess. Plus, I secretly hoped Sebastian couldn't say no to coming, and I wanted everything to be perfect. I wanted to share everything I had learned about Ai Po with him.

Mom was prepping lunch when I got home. Being my last day, she wanted to make my favorite: drunk chicken and sticky rice. I got hungry just smelling them even after all the croissants I had eaten.

"Mom, do you think you'll come to the Christmas gala? I want you to know I'm okay with you not going," though I really wasn't, "but I think you would really enjoy yourself. Cook is even preparing some Chinese meals. We're even going to have sticky rice cakes even though it's not Chinese New Year's yet. What do you think?"

"Anne, is it that important to you that I attend? You know I'm not into fine dining and fancy parties."

"It is important to me. It's my first one and I could really use your support."

"Then I'm going."

"Really? Just like that?"

"You are still my daughter even if you're stupid rich now," she said laughing.

"Would you come to Taiwan next year with me?"

"Not again, Anne," she said still laughing. "Eat your lunch."

Not wanting to push my luck I dropped the subject and enjoyed the rest of the afternoon with Mom.

23

THE HOUSE WAS GLOWING, and I stood outside in awe. I arrived back Sunday night thinking maybe I'd get a good night's sleep and start my week afresh. My eyes started tearing up as I looked around. It was so quiet and all the lights reflecting off the fresh snow made for a magical combination. The outline of the whole house was lit up and everything sparkled like fairies had landed and sprinkled their dust everywhere. Candles sparkled in every window and I felt like I was at my own version of the North Pole. I imagined Ai Po seeing this for the first time and being just as mesmerized.

"It's magical isn't it?" I looked to the left and saw Andy walking around the house. "I was just talking to Henry."

"It sure is. Henry? What are you doing out at this time?"

"He's one of the guys who takes care of maintenance. The horse stall has been needing some TLC for a while, and he started working on it today in order for everything to be in top shape by the gala."

"Why didn't you tell me? And shouldn't Ben be doing this stuff, especially this late?"

"I sent Ben to bed. He hasn't been feeling well, and I don't need a lot of sleep. You have sounded stressed on the phone so I didn't want to add to your worry. This is a simple enough thing for me to take care of. It's quite routine."

"Well, next time please let me know. I'd like to learn more about what goes on around here to take care of everything and everyone."

"Of course," he said still with no smile. I could tell he probably still wouldn't tell me. This was going to take some getting used to. I always knew everything that was going on in my life.

"Shall we go in? Your nose is starting to turn a bright red."

"Oh, yes, let's do." We walked into the foyer and I felt a weight roll down my shoulder. I was here again. It felt right to be back. I knew I had made the right decision.

"It is good to have you home," said Andy.

"It's very nice to be back, Andy."

"How is your mother?"

"She's doing great. She's completely ignoring everything I'm doing here though she said she would come to the gala. She doesn't want to talk about anything related to my grandmother."

"Change is hard. Give her some time. Let's get you settled in again. I'm sure you'll want to see how everything is going, but I'll follow up with you tomorrow morning. I'll let Cook know you're back and she will prep a breakfast for you in bed."

"That sounds fantastic, Andy. Thank you," I beamed. It felt so good to be taken care of by someone other than my mom. I was glad to be back.

I woke to rain outside my window which made me snuggle deeper into my covers and enjoyed that I was back in a house that I owned. Then I realized it was still early and it might be at least 30 minutes before Andy brought my food up. There was time to see if the next journal was in Ai Po's chest. I was learning so much about her personality and I felt guilty for thinking like this of my own Ai Po, but I wanted to know what happened next in my personal soap opera. Running over to the trunk, I was so excited to read, but *dang!* I forgot where I put the key. Paranoid about someone taking it, I put it in a different spot before I left, and of course, now I couldn't remember. All my usual places: drawers, under the mattress, inside books, behind pictures, inside my shoe, pockets of pants showed no signs of the key . . . *Where did I put the key?* Andy was going to be here in five minutes. *Oh well.* I needed to get dressed and would just have to continue looking while I had breakfast.

"Miss?" I turned to see half of Ben. He was trying not to peer into my room.

"I'm sorry, Miss, but Andy is asking you to come to the ballroom to help out with a certain matter. He and I both apologize that your breakfast wasn't able to be brought up. I brought you a croissant I found in the kitchen though. It's still warm," said Ben still hiding behind the door.

"Ben, it's okay, I'm dressed, but I'll be down to the ballroom in a few minutes."

"Great! I'll just put the croissant right here on the vanity," Ben said and then exited quickly.

Something must be up as they were both usually pretty chill about things. I got out of my pajamas and freshened up a bit, just so I didn't look like a complete monster. As I got closer to the ballroom, I heard bickering. Soon I heard what was being said, and it made me ill to think Andy was dealing with this and hadn't told me.

"You tell the lady that if she wants to put together this grand ball she better start answering our questions when we ask them. You might be okay with her leaving for a week, but we have a job to do, and we can't do it if she's not answering our questions. I am not pulling extra weight to hang something or string more lights just to have to redo it later so that her rich family and friends can enjoy it," said a voice behind the door.

"Us, too," said a couple other voices not as believing as the first one.

What in the world was happening? I thought he said everyone was doing great. I pushed the door open to see Andy standing with his back to me and three other workers facing him. It looked like an inquisition from the front person. Her face displayed every level of unhappiness while the other two cowered behind her.

"Anne has the right to go see her mother when she wants and continue with her job. That is not for us to say. She is the master of this household. Some answers could wait until she came back."

I pushed the door further open and all the eyes turned to look at me. Immediately, everything went silent. Hostile eyes looked me up and down while the others looked down in embarrassment that they were a part of this. I was about to say something when Andy started talking again.

"As you can see, Anne is back. She just got back yesterday and Ben and I plan on catching her up with everything that has been going on. I think I can safely say that Anne came back to focus on the task at hand."

"Yes, of course. I'm back, and I will stay through the gala, if not longer, and I felt bad for being away for as long as I was."

"Great. I think we should all get back to what we were doing. Anne, will you please come with me," Andy said before I could get another word out. The whole situation made me feel uncomfortable, but I followed Andy back to his office. Andy, Ben, and I talked for the next hour about all the details that still needed to be done, the unhappiness of the one staff member at having to rush to get this gala together, and for me not being here. This last point Andy said was just because I was new. Lord Anthony and Sir Anthony were not here for a lot of the planning as well, but they had also been putting the gala on for many years so the staff trusted them and knew what they wanted without thinking. I was a new beast to them, and they couldn't read me, so they were getting frustrated waiting for Andy to call me for answers before moving on to their next task. Anything from color choices for the tablecloths, should this extra person be invited, which room will be for which family member . . . I found out there were items that had to be ordered or made specifically for certain guests because they were very particular about the wine or food they ate. Decisions had to be made. This one particular staff member apparently complained a lot as well, and I was not to engage with her, but show her I was the head of this household. I was so glad I had decided to come back. The rest of the day I talked to different staff members and got a tour of the place. Apparently, family members were going to start arriving over the weekend for the gala the following Thursday on Christmas Eve.

❄ 24 ❄

FRESH SNOW the day before Christmas Eve! Outside my window was the view of the fountain and the long driveway that seemed forever ago I first drove in on. I would never get tired of this view. Andy had told me that basically everything was done. Guests had been arriving since Sunday. Mostly cousins of Sir Anthony, but they kept to themselves, though I would always catch their eyes following me when I walked by. Cook was working all the time, and her age was starting to show, but these cousins were very demanding about having the finest food and drinks. The kitchen was my sanctuary, and I frequented there so I could save up all of my energy for socializing at the gala. Sebastian still hadn't RSVP'd, and I was getting nervous. Victoria said she was coming, and I was so excited and happy about that.

We were all excited about tomorrow, but today I was going to take advantage and read Ai Po's next journal. The key had been taped to the back of my mattress. Clearly, I wanted to find a new hiding place and was a bit too good at it. Finally, after more than a week, I was going to curl up and enjoy the next saga in her life. My thoughts went to my mom for a second hoping she would come tonight. I had invited her over to stay the night, so she could be here all day tomorrow through the weekend, but she only said maybe and didn't say anything else. It flummoxed me why she was acting this way.

I sat in my closet, opened the chest, and breathed in the smell of mustiness. Mothballs. My mom loved using them and she said she had learned to use them from her mom. It was very distinctive and felt like a comforting blanket. I looked at the red qipao in a different light. My Ai Po's dress from her lover. She cherished it all these years. Curious, I quickly stripped, and the dress slid right on. It was like it was made for me. I turned to face the mirror and gasped. The dress was beautiful in itself, but even more striking on. A high collar hugged my neck with a small opening in front. Two floral pankous held the top together one at the neck and one on the right collarbone. The red made my hair stand out and maybe I would look even better for Sebastian if I just added some color to my face. Suddenly, I realized that I didn't have Victoria here to help me with my makeup. I was going to have a beautiful dress, but no makeup and no idea what to do with my hair. The little that she had taught me seemed rudimentary, but I would have to do what I could. I changed back into my pajamas because, try as I might, I was afraid to sit on the floor in the dress. It was not the most movable thing to wear if you wanted to be comfortable. Hanging it up, I made a note to ask Andy if he could have it steamed. I found the next journal and made myself comfortable amongst the pillows. Now I really wanted some hot chocolate and a cozy fireplace. Nope, people would find me too easily. I opened to the first page:

36年1月29日 (Wednesday, January 29, 1947)

I'm sorry I have been AWOL (as the Americans like to say), but I have been living a dream. It's a struggle to keep our relationship a secret, but I understand why we have to. I'm bursting to tell you what has been going on in the last month. I taught him Chinese every day, sometimes in the library and sometimes on our bench. He was a fast learner, and we were starting to have simple conversations all in Chinese. At the same time, he was also teaching me English, and we could converse—he in Chinese and me in English—and actually carry on like this for full conversations. After our kiss the day of the gala, we have done much more kissing everywhere. He sometimes sneaks into my room at night, or we find a dark space in the library. I had no idea my body could feel the way he makes me feel or do the things we have done. And oh, the sensations he brings out in me is beyond my expectations. I know our relationship is taboo, and I've seen Andy lurking around giving me concerned looks at times, but we are covering our tracks and I'm the happiest I have ever been in my life. I don't want this to end, and I'm just going with the flow. What could possibly go wrong except that he drops me for someone else? I'm not stupid to think that a man of his stature only has me, but he sure does know how to make me feel special. Lord Anthony gives me his stern stare every once in a while, but I just feel sorry for him that he isn't happier.

Ai Po had sex when she was seventeen! And mom always made such a big deal that I couldn't even have a boyfriend until college!

36年2月14日 (Friday, February 14, 1947)

Anthony sent me chocolates and gave me earrings though I can't fathom when I'd be able to wear them. He said today was their Valentine's Day, and I was his valentine. What am I going to do? I think I'm falling in love with him. I can't fall in love with him. He's way beyond my level. I didn't think I would fall in love with someone like him. I'm just a lowly seamstress and he's the heir to a fortune. He can have anyone he wants. It's been all fun and games, but my heart has started to ache when I see him around others, and I am pretending he doesn't know me as well as he does. I must keep up this charade in order to still be with him. I can't talk to Andy or Cook about any of this and definitely not my parents. On a happier note, he has continued leaving notes for me in the bench every day. Sometimes they are short poems he has written about me, a drawing that he did of me from memory, always with plum blossoms in the corner, and on occasion, it will be a long letter telling me about his day and all the tasks he has to do, and the expectations of his father. I don't hear him talk about his mother and sisters as much. He seems to get along with his brother quite well and takes him on most of his outings. Sometimes I feel like I know his mom and sisters better than he does. He's so scared of his father, but at the same time respects him. I couldn't imagine losing face in front of my father, which exacerbates the situation I have put myself in by falling in love with Anthony. Father would never approve and I know he would call me a silly girl. Unappreciative of everything he and Mom have done for me. I can hear him yelling at me, but I wouldn't change anything and it's too late, anyway. He also told me he made a blossom notch in his bed frame in order to "see" me before he goes to sleep. I was so flattered I didn't know what to say. I blushed when he wiped away snow from my face and kissed me on the temple while holding me close. I don't know how I'll live without this man in my life.

36年2月21日 (Friday, February 21, 1947)

You are now my only friend. It's not hard to keep myself busy as there is plenty of work around the house if I'm not sewing, but I can't talk to anyone. I've also been feeling very tired lately and I'm not sure why. I'm not sure what to write in here anymore because it's all the same. I focus on preparing our Chinese lessons, and Anthony is absorbing everything I say. He is also looking tired these days. I think the stress of our relationship is also weighing on him as well. His father has been pulling him into more and more meetings. He thinks his father wants him to take over the company sooner than he thought. He doesn't feel ready, and he's not sure he wants to. He loves art so much, but that doesn't make a living and doesn't live up to his family's expectations. I understand his feelings as I did not have a choice in my profession as well. My family is not rich like his, but we were both put into the same situation of our family business. He has started carving gifts for me. He is so artistic and gifted with his hands. It's sad to me that he is not allowed to pursue his passion because it does not align with his family. He would produce such great artwork that would benefit many. I wish we were both in different situations and could really be there for each other. At least we have each other as confidants now.

Then the entries stopped. There were what looked like remnants of tape residue on some of the following pages, but I wasn't sure. Then I found the entries started again about 20 pages later. It was dated a month later and her hands had been shaking when writing it.

"Anne..."

"Oh, my god, you scared me," I said jumping up and sending the journal flying through the air and hitting Andy on the head.

"I'm so sorry! Are you okay?" I ran over to see if I had permanently damaged the head of a 78-year-old man.

"I'm okay, it was not a hard landing. Very sorry, I tried knocking from the main door to the room, but no one answered. I thought you might be here in the closet so I came in just to check. I should have knocked before entering," said Andy looking humiliated.

"It's quite all right. I was just startled. I was so engrossed in my grandmother's journal I probably would not have noticed the knock. I can put all of this away and come help with whatever is needed."

"No, we are done for tomorrow or as far as we can go without the guests here. I thought you would like to see the visitor that is here."

"Visitor?"

"Yes, he said for me not to tell you who it was, but for you to come down and meet him."

"Him?" *Why was I answering in one word questions?* But all of a sudden I got hot and bothered. It couldn't be Sebastian. Why would he show up now if he could just come tomorrow, but what if it was? I was still in my pajamas, hadn't combed my hair, or washed my face. My breath smelled disgusting.

"I can let him know you will be down in a bit. You are just finishing up your task?" asked Andy. Sometimes it seemed Andy could read my mind.

"Yes, yes, that would be great. Let me freshen up and I'll be down in ten minutes."

"Take your time. He is not in a hurry." As Andy retreated, I put the journals back in the trunk. This time, I made sure I had the key on me and went back to the room to freshen up. The whole time I thought my heart would jump out of my body. I hurried out and made myself take deep breaths to calm down before I turned the corner to walk down the stairs. I was shocked when I saw who it was. I had totally forgotten about him.

"Anne, it's so good to see you again. I hope this is not a total surprise. Based on your face, it seems you were expecting someone else," said Jack. His eyes gleamed with mischievousness and he looked genuinely happy to see me. I immediately calmed down and was equally happy to see him as well.

"It's so good to see you!"

"You haven't thought of me since the reading have you?" he said, but I could tell he was half joking. "You look like you've started settling into your new house."

"I love this house. There's so much history to it."

"There's definitely history here. More than you'll ever know," he said looking around him at all the carvings. "Glad to hear you're enjoying yourself."

"Are you hungry, thirsty? Do you want me to get you anything?"

"No, I'm all set. Andy or Cook can always whip up my favorite and take care of me. Goodness knows, I practically grew up with the two of them." Oh, that's right. I forgot he lived here, too. "I came early today to see you."

"Me?" Again with the one-word responses.

"I wanted to gauge how you were doing before my family descended on your new house. And truthfully, I am in for some light entertainment. At my age, I look for fun wherever I can get it."

"Fun?" I was starting to get nervous about where all this was going.

"Yes, fun. My family you met at the reading were only the main contenders. The others: cousins, extended cousins, aunts, uncles, relatives I probably don't even know about are all coming tomorrow. There have been phone calls to me asking for more details about you," he held up his hand as if to calm me. "To which I say I know nothing, and that all I've heard is that you are a wonderful person and the rightful heir to the house and fortune. Then they usually hang up. It's all quite amusing to me, and I cannot wait to see what happens tomorrow. By the way, why would you put together this gala right after you inherited the house? I can only imagine you have no idea what you're getting yourself into."

"Clearly, I don't." I regained some of my composure. Apparently, I was going to be Exhibit A at my own gala, but I should have known that. "I don't know what I was thinking except that I wanted to continue something Sir Anthony loved. I love Christmas and it seemed the perfect thing to allow the staff, family, friends, and me to meld together."

"Well, maybe that's how your family does Christmas. With ours, it's more of a competition and business opportunity gesture on who can out-dress, out-talk, and outdo the other person in order to gain more popularity or status in the hierarchy that you will see tomorrow. You being Chinese, unfortunately, will play into the whole mix as well. Some know and some don't. I believe some think it's just a rumor and are hoping you look and act just like them. I'm sure Andy already had you memorize all the people who are coming and where they are in the hierarchy?"

"Yes," I groaned. It had really opened my eyes to this new world I'd been thrown into.

"Well, it's not all bad. The staff here is the best and as long as you treat them fairly they will do what you ask and help when needed. There are some in the family who are decent. And you have me," he said with a big grin on his face.

"Well, so far all you've done is make me feel worse about everything and told me that I'm to be your amusement for tomorrow. That makes me feel grand," I threw back at him.

"Yes, yes, I'm sorry about that. I haven't had a family event I've been so excited to attend in many years if not for over a decade. I miss my brother dearly and wish you could have known him in person. He was my favorite person and genuinely decent compared to all his other relatives. I tried to copy him wherever I could. I am at your service, Anne. Do not ever doubt. I am on your side," he said with a serious look.

"Thank you, Jack. I really appreciate this," I said, not knowing what else to say. This was too much for me to process the day before the gala. I was more nervous than before, and every cell in my body wanted to go restudy the list of people coming, so I would have some control over who I was talking to tomorrow. For a person who kept to herself, I was going to be thrown into the limelight, and it was all my fault.

"I have clearly made you more nervous than you already were. Let's ask Cook to dish up some of her cake and go walk in the garden. I haven't seen this house in ages and the snow makes it so magical."

"How do you know Cook has cake?"

"Cook always has cake. If you don't already know that, then you have not been paying attention to the details of this household. Open your eyes and ears and you will learn much."

"I knew she has cake all the time," I sulked. I knew about the cake and wasn't sure why I was surprised that Jack knew, but it still threw me that he grew up here. The house was basically empty when I moved in so the connections and history of this place kept surprising me. He was right, though, that I had been so absorbed in my own thoughts and learnings that I hadn't been paying attention to a lot of the details of this household. I vowed to do just that moving forward. It did me no good to not know my own home as well as I knew my mother's.

"Are you joining?" asked Jack already halfway to the kitchen.

"Yes, coming." In my new bewildered state, I followed behind Jack hoping he really meant what he said, that he was on my side. I was becoming terrified about who I was going to be meeting the next day.

25

SLEEP ELUDED ME LAST NIGHT. It was like a thousand rocks had settled in my stomach and wouldn't let up. Grinding and churning and moving to my shoulders, so I felt like I was pinned to my bed, which I was happy to stay in, but I was the host. I made myself get up and saw a note that someone slid under my door.

Hot coffee and breakfast are right outside your door. Today will be excellent. You have the morning to yourself. We will find you at 2:00 to do a walk-through of the grounds. The guests will start arriving around 6:00. We are here when you need us. - Andy and Ben

Dear old Andy, I don't know what I would have done these many weeks without him. Ben had been equally there, too, and supportive. I'm glad that he was learning everything from Andy. As I made myself eat breakfast, I thought about everything Jack had said. He and I had eaten our weight in cake and walked through the gardens talking about my guests. He gave me some pointers on how to speak to certain uncles and cousins that he knew would be showing up. What really caused me alarm was he said I shouldn't be surprised if some of them brought up subjects that only certain people in my life would know. Certain cousins were nosy and probably hired a private eye to investigate me in order for them to see who they were up against. He couldn't tell me what this information might be, but who goes and investigates someone!?

I went down to see Cook. She said I could come visit her whenever I wanted if things got too crazy for me, and it already was, but I was going to get through this. At least, that's what I kept telling myself. How hard could it be compared to landing in a new country and rebuilding my life with new people, new customs, and new surroundings?

"Did you like the frittatas I made for you this morning? The mushrooms were just delivered fresh this morning and I couldn't wait to use them," asked Cook as I walked down the stairs.

"They were delicious as always, and I still can't believe how early you wake up to start cooking."

"Wait till you taste the menu we have been pouring over the last few weeks."

"I cannot believe we spent so much time on just food. All the allergies, food preferences, dietary constraints. I'd think that the Queen was coming into town."

"Anne, you have to understand the Queen might as well be. The guests that are coming are Sir Anthony's closest relatives, by blood, not because he actually talked to them. If they aren't family, they are his closest business partners, and within this big group of people, a few of them are his dear, dear friends. You are to wow them today and the food will go a long way to do just that."

"Ugh, I'm so in over my head. Why didn't any of you talk me out of this?"

"What would be the fun in that? You were new to us and yes, some wanted to see how much you could handle, but some, like me, knew you could do it. You wouldn't have moved into a foreign place if you couldn't. You will need to learn the ways of the house and know the connections that come with the house at some point. What better point than now? And we love the gala. Sir Anthony always took care of us during the holidays and it was a beautiful time to be here."

"Ah! Take care of you all. I haven't paid you all your bonus. Do I give you guys time off?"

"Anne," said Cook laughing at me. She seemed to be in high spirits today even with the workload that she was going to have to do. "Andy has already taken care of it. I would just talk to him to make sure you understand for next year, but other than that, there's no need to worry yourself about it right now. You have a gala to host," said Cook as she flung her hands high up in the air to show the grandioseness of the event.

"I'm going to go for a walk in the garden and enjoy my morning before everyone starts showing up. Quick question, though. What do you know about Jack?"

"Jack. He was always in the shadows of Sir Anthony, but Sir Anthony loved him very much and always took care of him. Jack lived a simple life compared to the rest of his family. He was still very well off, but he definitely did not go around showing off his money like some of his sisters and their families ended up doing. I feel shame for Sir Anthony and his father every time I think of the sisters. They always had to have the finest. But I deter. Jack likes jokes and fun. I would watch out for him over-promising, but overall, I trust him. He means well, and would be someone you should get to know."

"Thanks, Cook. That's good to know."

My mom arrived around 11 o'clock and she seemed nervous, too. It just made me more nervous about the whole day. She was my rock support, and I needed her. Cook made us the best lamb and rice dish, and I was able to walk with her through the garden and show her the statues. She was silent the whole walk, but she seemed to listen to me as I told her about what I had learned over the last few weeks. I was glad she had come.

Promptly at 2 o'clock, Andy and Ben came and got us. Mom followed us as we walked around the house. She was wide-eyed looking at the transformation of the whole house. The entryway showed off the 15-foot Christmas tree at the top of the stairs. Garlands wrapped along the entire staircase as well as the columns on the second floor. Candles in every window, mistletoe above the library door, and Christmas lights tastefully placed to light up the entryway, hallways, and of course, the outside of the house. The four of us sat on the fountain at the front of the house and just looked out at the surroundings.

"Anne, I say this as much for you as for your mom to hear, too. Remember you are your own person and you have made quite an impression on the staff here. I have known this family for more years than I've known my own parents. Many of the staff only knew the rich and famous that frequented this doorstep. For you to come in as our master and to be kind and generous toward everyone has shown who you are. Many of the staff members will need time to warm up more, but most can see that you are not here to change things or ruin people's lives. Remember that today when you meet your guests. They are your guests and this is your home. You are the rightful owner and not them. Ms. Lin, you have raised a wonderful daughter and both of you are more than worthy to be living here," said Andy with so much endearment in his voice that I almost cried. My mom did tear. She grabbed my hand.

"Andy, it is nice to hear you say this about my daughter. I know that I've been acting strangely. I'm sorry, Anne, I have not been here for you the last few weeks. Stories your Ai Po told me have been coming up, and it has all been very overwhelming for me to see all of this and hear you talk about the journals. Anne, you have done a wonderful job here. The place looks amazing and I know you will wow the people coming today who are looking for you to flop. This is —or was—not our world, but you will make it your own. I am too old for all of this, but I am here for you tonight," said my mom through tear-filled eyes. I gave her a big hug and didn't let her go.

"Thank you. Mom, I hope you have a wonderful time tonight. You deserve it. I'm so glad you came. And why haven't you ever mentioned these stories of Grandma?" I asked, giving her my best stern face.

"Now is not the time. Another day, Anne," and before I could object, Andy pulled us all up and told us we should probably go get dressed.

She surprised me when she pulled out a beautiful black evening gown and said that Grandma had made it for her when she was courting Dad, and they had gone to a black and white ball. Before I could ask why she kept it as she had gotten rid of everything else associated with Dad, she said she couldn't get herself to give it away or throw away when it was the last memento she had of her mom. It was almost like it was a parting gift before Grandma left us. I had never seen it before and was glad Mom had chosen to wear it tonight. It looked stunning on her with cap sleeves and a sweetheart line across the front. It went all the way down to her feet and she seemed actually comfortable in it. Mom gasped when I put on Grandma's qipao. She almost cried but caught herself just in time before her makeup started running.

"Anne, you are the strongest girl I know. Hold your head up amongst all these guests of ours, and remember you are the host, not anyone else."

"Thanks, Mom. It's really nice to hear you say this. Doesn't make me less nervous though."

Just then the doorbell rang. How it was 6 o'clock already was beyond me, but I took a deep breath and Mom and I walked down the stairs together to greet our guests.

❧ 26 ❧

I DIDN'T KNOW what everyone was so worried about. All the guests were lovely and super nice to me. They all seemed to know each other, and it appeared many of them had not seen each other in a long time so a lot of happy faces floated around. Just like in Ai Po's entry, I couldn't believe the wealth of gowns, jewelry, and suits that were being flaunted about. I couldn't care less about what I wore every day, and I had no social life, but I wasn't oblivious to fashion and today I witnessed every fashion trend I could think of in real life right in front of me. It was like my own personal catwalk, but completely immersive. I had to keep reminding myself I was the hostess, and I couldn't just be a fly on the wall. It was hard to smile, shake hands, nod, and even throw out an opinion every once in a while that wasn't the same comment over and over again. My mom had stuck by my side for the first couple of hours. She and I would compare notes on people's outfits in between meeting people. She would even get me a couple hors d'oeuvres from the table, so I didn't faint, but she retired early and said she had had enough. I was very self-conscious after that, my brain was getting tired fast, and my stomach was growling so loud I think some of the guests heard it. The table kept getting closer, but I would get stopped every step I made. It was worse because I knew what was being served, and I had been looking forward to the food all week. Cook had said she'd save me some food to eat after the gala or if I wanted to sneak away to eat it, but I couldn't get away and I was hungry now. Next time, I would eat the food she saved before the gala.

"Anne, is it?"

I turned with the biggest smile I could muster ready to go into my conversational mode again, hating that I had to force myself.

"Yes, that's me."

"So good to finally meet you. I was curious how your night is going?"

"It's going very well. Everyone has been very kind, and it's been really nice to meet everyone. Are you Sir Walter?"

"Ha! I see Andy has been prepping you properly. Jack told me not to take you for granted. Yes, I am Sir Walter. Please just call me Walter. The whole title thing was my wife's doing and I've never liked it. I apologize I was not able to make the will reading, but Geraldine seemed to have represented our family quite well, and I'm sure my daughter, Jacqueline, made her impression on you. My granddaughter, Isabella, should be here as well. She's a sweet girl, but very much like her mother." He said all this without a hint of irony or sarcasm. Part of me wanted to say the truth about the impression they gave me, but I knew this was not the time. I knew who he was from Andy's dossier, but I sure didn't know the man himself. For the first time tonight I was nervous, but I reminded myself that I had nothing to be afraid of. This wasn't anything I couldn't handle.

"Yes, I did meet your wife and daughter at the will reading. We were only there for maybe thirty minutes, so I wasn't able to get to know them very well. I'm sorry to have missed you, too."

"Oh, you were not missing anything. I think Jack was the best person for you to meet. This might not be PC in this day and age, but at my age, I couldn't care less anymore. Your Grandma was one good-looking woman for a Chinese person in those days. Exotic, confident, different. Something people desired. I know we were all a bit jealous that my brother-in-law won, but he was always the charmer. But you know how the saying goes, lovers are fun and all, but they come and go. Well, it looks like I'm being called from across the room by what looks like my wife, so I will be heading off. Nice to meet you. Don't bother trying to get in touch with me. My wife will probably never tell me if you called, and well, I'm just useless." With that, he turned and swayed his way through the crowd. My mouth dropped open and I couldn't get myself to close it. Did I just hear what I think I heard about my Ai Po. Is that what people thought of her? I knew I'd been reading about her love with Sir Anthony, but nothing in there had given me the impression that she was wanted by all, and that Sir Anthony "won"—as if she was a prize. Shock started turning into anger and frustration, and I knew I had to exit before it boiled over.

I wandered down the hall and ended up in the sitting room where it was nice and quiet. There was a young couple in the corner being all touchy-feely, but at least the focus was not on me. It would be the perfect hideaway while I got my head screwed on again. Then I heard loud voices coming from the other direction, and before I could leave, an entourage of people in their 20s stumbled in. They looked like really close friends or cousins. A pang of jealousy shot through me wondering where Victoria was. They were hanging onto each other with arms intertwined. One of them looked like an exact duplicate of Jacqueline. Definitely looked like they had been doing something they shouldn't have at the back of the house.

"Anne! There you are. We have been looking for you all night. This party is outrageous. I couldn't have put on a better party if I tried. I heard all about you from my mom. She wasn't very impressed with you, but I told her that we had to give you a chance. We can't just assume that someone like you couldn't run the family business. You Oriental people are supposed to be super smart right?" At this, the others all laughed. "I'm sorry, I can't stay, I'm supposed to be looking for my grandparents to say hi to. I'm sure both are creating quite the scene upstairs. These are my cousins: Bernice, Kevin, Jessica, Lauren, Peter, and Emily. Have a great time. Ciao!" And she exited while blowing a kiss to everyone. I stood there stunned. Everyone else stared at me like I was a specimen. Some had smirks on their faces and some just looked bored. I pushed through my fear, braced myself, and reined in my anger.

"So, you're the girl who inherited the fortune. You do look quite ordinary. There's a rumor flying around that your grandmother and Sir Anthony had quite the affair and almost toppled the family fortune," said Bernice.

"I heard she was a common chink who was after fame and fortune. I don't blame her. She probably had it all calculated before she got off the boat, but looks like she got her riches two generations too late."

"That is not true and I don't appreciate you spreading rumors about my family when you don't even know them," I spat out while I felt my face turning red. So much for reining in my anger. I couldn't believe what they just said about her! Did they really call her that?

"Is it true that your father passed away when you were twelve?" asked Jessica.

"How—? Who . . . ?" I found myself turning my head back and forth between all of them not sure who to focus on at this point.

"I heard your friend hasn't even been around to share this with you. She's off having fun exploring herself in Europe. And your mom's art only makes ends meet, and she's so frightened by something that she won't even set foot here," said Bernice. This all came out so fast I had a hard time collecting my thoughts. How did they know all of this? My whole body was shaking.

"My mother is here today and I don't know how or who told you all of this, but it's not based on truth, and I would appreciate you leaving now."

"Oh, don't worry about how or who. And no need to get defensive. This is the price you pay for getting rich. You're everyone's business now. It's really quite interesting to me. Poor girl inherits riches because her ancestor fell in love with the right person. A rags-to-riches story and you didn't even have to do a thing. I can't wait to see what happens to you," said Kevin, and they laughed and stumbled out into the hallway. Lauren, Peter, and Emily hadn't said a word this whole time and looked embarrassed as they walked away with the group.

I sat down on the cushions not knowing what just happened. Tears were threatening to come out, but I also knew I couldn't just leave the party. I was the hostess, and the staff had worked so hard to put this together. But boy did I want to just find a hole and hide from everyone. Served me right for getting comfortable in this new life of mine. I was so naïve. The sound of feet approaching made me pull myself together to exit the room. But it was Andy.

"Anne, are you okay? You look like you've just received terrible news. Please sit."

"Oh, Andy, you warned me that people might say nasty things tonight. But I only half believed you," I said through tears that were starting to leak down my face and ruin all my makeup. Makeup that Betsy had tediously put on me after watching me try to put it on myself.

"I was afraid of this, but know that Sir Anthony chose you, not them. Plus there is a surprise at the door waiting for you."

"What is it?"

"Not what but who. Come."

I followed Andy to the entrance and ran into Sebastian's arms forgetting that I wasn't going to cry.

"Well, hello to you, too. I see I've been missed," Sebastian said while holding me close. "Why don't we head into the library? Andy, how is the party going?"

"The party is going splendidly. There is nothing to worry about. Anne has done her rounds for the last few hours so I don't think she will be missed," Andy said winking at us.

Sebastian brought me into the library, and I sat down across from him. He motioned for me to sit next to him, but I stayed put. I didn't know why I did this. We sat there not talking for a while, waiting for others to leave, and filling the awkward silence between the two of us with more awkwardness. I finally got the courage to speak up.

"I loved the roses you sent." He sat in front of me with one arm on the back of the sofa and the other on his leg. Always confident Sebastian.

"Only the finest for you."

"Oh, don't get me started. I don't need all the fine things," I said with more bitterness than I meant.

"Whoa, that changed courses fast."

"Sorry, I just had some people who got under my skin. I'm glad I have you as a friend."

"See, there's the problem. Friends. I've been thinking this week. I don't think I can be friends with you, Anne," he said with the most serious face. I sat there and just stared at him not sure what to say to that. Had I read him wrong that he wanted to get to know me?

"Is that why you haven't called all week?"

"Now, before your mind goes off into a million directions, I can't be friends with you because I've developed what romantics like to call feelings for you," he said with still the same serious face. "Trust me. I've tried to get rid of these feelings as you just aren't my type, but something about you has really grabbed me and I don't want to let it go," he continued.

Did Sebastian just say he liked me? This was more than I expected. "Well, I don't know if I should be flattered right now or annoyed that I would make you want to not feel," was the best comeback I could think of.

Then he burst out laughing. "Always so serious."

"I propose that we get out of this stuffy house and out into the gardens. I can show you some new statues I've found," avoiding the subject for as long as I could.

"That would be great. By the way, have you still been reading your grandmother's journals?"

"Yes. I had just gotten to a really interesting part yesterday, and I haven't been able to pick it up again."

"I'd love to read more with you if that's okay," he looked at me with pleading eyes.

"Yes, that would be great. Let me just go get the next one." As I ran up the stairs, I thought to myself that I might like him back as well and that made me smile. I almost forgot about the unpleasant encounter earlier. Almost.

We went out to the garden and followed the lit path. It was very romantic, and we walked in silence for a while. I showed him the tree and the new statues I had found. At one point he pulled me in close and gave me a tight hug. It felt so nice to be in his arms, and we walked like that for a while. Turning a corner, I thought I saw a shadow coming from behind us, but when I turned to look there was no one there, and I scolded myself for being paranoid. We ended up back under the plum blossom tree sitting in silence while I opened the journal and started to translate.

36年3月19日 (Wednesday, March 19, 1947)
    We've been discovered! I don't know what I'm going to do now.
    My life is ruined, and all because I was stubborn and wanted to have
    my love that I knew was forbidden.

"Goodness, what have you been reading since I last saw you?" Sebastian looked at me with horrified eyes. "The last time I read it she was doing great and in a new household."

"You've been gone for a week. A lot has happened." I felt awful for snapping at him, but Ai Po was in love with someone she shouldn't be for all sorts of reasons, and the rude encounter earlier still bothered me. All sorts of feelings had come up this week, and I wasn't sure about being with someone from a different race. That thought surprised me. I hadn't thought I had a problem with that before.

"Okay, okay, let's keep reading," he gently pleaded as we readjusted ourselves on the bench.

Lord Anthony found out about Anthony and me. We don't know who told on us when we've been very careful about where we meet and what we do, but everything is out in the open now. Lady Mary intervened, so I've been locked in my room and only Lord Anthony has the key, but I wasn't kicked out of the house just yet. I thought I saw a hint of pity in her eyes, but she might just want her dresses done. Her daughter, Bernice, is getting married, and I had just started on her dress, and I know she has been bragging about it. Everyone has been told not to talk to me. I'm no longer going to get the check that was coming to me, food comes through a crack and then the door is quickly closed, and I can hear imitations of fake Chinese being spoken outside my door and then laughing.

Lord Anthony called me into his office this morning. I was scared as he never calls me in. I've heard stories of servants being called in and leaving in tears because they were fired. I can't be fired. He got straight to the point. Someone had recently told him that his son had been spending a lot of time with me. More so than just tutoring. That they had seen us sneaking around at night. I was so red in the face I couldn't look at him. It was all I could do to keep the tears forming in my eyes from falling down my face. I was shaking all over. He started raising his voice. Suddenly, he sat down and started talking in a controlled and even voice, which was scarier than the yelling. He asked if I knew how much it took for him to hire an Oriental. That this was the way I showed gratitude toward him and his family for saving my family from poverty. How dare I hoodwink his son! He told me to head to my room and pack as I was to leave immediately. I wanted to run and run I did. I bolted for the door and ran to the stairs. Suddenly, I tripped over my feet trying to fly down the stairs to my room to grab everything and make a break for it. The last thing I remembered was seeing the steps racing before my eyes and Anthony running in yelling my name. I woke on a hospital bed groggy and strapped like a criminal. I had to pee so badly. The door was cracked open, and I saw people moving about outside. I started to yell for help, but then I saw the back of Lord Anthony and a man dressed all in white conversing right outside the door. They must have thought I was still asleep because they didn't bother to lower their voices. I almost wished I hadn't heard them. The doctor told Lord Anthony that my leg was sprained very badly, but not broken, and besides the fracture in my wrist, I only had bruises over the rest of my body. I heard Lord Anthony say I would survive as if he didn't care one way or the other. Then the doctor said he found out something extra that Lord Anthony should know about: That I was pregnant! I was about a month along. I heard Lord Anthony say to get rid of it. That this will teach the Orient her rightful place. I was in so much shock I couldn't think straight. They put some sort of mask over me that made me go back to sleep. I woke up bandaged and bruised and hurting all over, but I was back in my room at the house, and as I said earlier, I've been locked in my room. I've been sitting here crying knowing I went into the hospital with a child inside me from the person I love and now I was empty. I didn't have either of them. I was alone. I don't know what Lord Anthony will do to me. I don't know where I will go. I think I had secretly wished that because Sir Anthony was the son that he would protect me, but he probably has no say in the matter. His father is all-consuming.

Tears were flowing down my face. I couldn't stop them. Sebastian had his arms around me and every once in a while I felt him squeeze my shoulders.

36年3月21日 (Friday, March 21, 1947)

I've been in my room for two days now. Apparently, they do not want me dead as Andy and Cook have slipped me food and toiletries at random times during the day. Neither will look at me, but leave what they've brought and hurry away. Anthony has come by a couple times and tried to talk to me through the door, but I don't want to talk to him. I've heard him crying and apologizing, and he even slipped me a note under the door but I remained silent, though inside I wanted to throw myself into his arms and have him tell me that everything would be okay. The doctor has come to visit me once and gave me some medication to get me through the pain. He also would not look at me but treated me like a rag doll. He placed a paper in my hand and asked me to read it later, but I haven't bothered to look at it. I hear whispering outside my door all the time, and I just know I'm the talk of the house if not the neighborhood. It reminds me of the town I came from where everyone was in everyone's business. The difference being then I would keep my head down and do my work. Now, I overstepped my boundaries and became too confident. I've learned my lesson. I hope they just leave me here for the rest of my life, so I do not need to show my shame to anyone, especially my family.

36年3月23日 (Sunday, March 23, 1947)

The most humiliating part of this whole thing was a letter was sent to my family telling them about my downfall. A letter from my father came back and I could practically hear him screaming at me through the paper. I couldn't dare show my face to them ever again. My door was unlocked shortly after lunchtime, and I was about to sit back and stare at the ceiling some more. I had started seeing shapes and was telling myself a story based on the characters I saw above. A couple staff members came in—once again not looking at me—grabbed my suitcase from below my bed and threw all of my items in it not caring if things were breakable, wrinkled, or even mine. I went around collecting the things they missed and took out the notes from under my mattress when they weren't looking and stuffed them into my suitcase. I'm glad I only had one hiding spot as I was out of the room as quickly as they had come in. Good thing I kept myself dressed at all times seeing how the family had a habit of barging into my room whenever they pleased. At the entrance, I stopped cold and had to be dragged to the front door. Lord and Lady Wilkens, their three daughters, both sons, and all the staff were standing at the entrance. Lady Mary somehow persuaded her husband to give me my last paycheck before sending me away. I had to stand in front of the whole staff while he made a great declaration of how he was being a great man and being very generous after what I had done. Anthony looked close to tears, and my first instinct was to run to him and wipe them off his face. To have his arms envelop me and tell me everything would be okay, but I held my ground. Everyone else, including the staff who was congregated in the background, looked inquisitive or had a righteous look on their face as if I was a rat they had found and was finally able to expel out of their household. Someone grabbed me by the arm and pulled me into the car. I only turned back once and saw Anthony standing at the top of the stairs with both arms clenched to his side as if he had been stopped mid-run with Lord Wilkens' hands firmly gripping his shoulder. Maybe he did love me. I went into the car and vowed to do everything I could to make this up to my family.

I couldn't read anymore. I was bawling by this time, and Sebastian was fully embracing me and rocking me back and forth. How could she be treated like this? Yes, she was a servant. Yes, she fell in love with the boss's son, which was taboo, but how can a human treat another human with so little care? She couldn't even depend on her own family. I felt Sebastian put his hand on my chin and lift my face up to his. I looked into his eyes and saw my own sorrow reflecting back at me. It was comforting to know someone else was sharing my pain as well. Before I knew it his lips were on mine and the warmth of his lips sent a warmth through me, and for the first time in my life, I felt like I had finally found a comforting place to be.

❧ 27 ❧

I ENDED up crying in his arms for some time. Long enough for him to walk me back to my room, tuck me into bed, and kiss me goodnight. He said something about checking on me tomorrow, but maybe that was just my mind wanting something that was too good to be true.

I looked in the mirror when I woke up to see that my eyes were puffy and red and I just wanted to crawl back under the covers. When I started reading Ai Po's journals, I never believed I would ever see her suffer the way she had. I naively imagined her living her life in the 1940s like I lived my life in the 2000s. An independent woman who could call her own shots. Yes, I knew women in the 1940s were treated very differently, but she had the disadvantage of being Chinese as well. This was my first time to have first-hand experience looking into an actual person's life in the 1940s and it was my own Ai Po! Even these days I still felt that I didn't belong in certain places. I couldn't imagine what she felt. What happened to her after this incident? How did my mother get conceived? How come I never really got to meet her? So many questions and I only hoped she kept writing in her journal and I would find them in the trunk.

Without much care to the rest of the world, I buried myself back into my covers and hoped I was not needed today. I could only hope the gala was a success. After the rude cousins of Isabella, my Ai Po's downfall, and my confusion about the things Sebastian said yesterday, I just did not want to face the world for the next twenty-four hours. However, that wasn't going to be the case. The doorbell rang, and two minutes later, a knock on my door. I groaned. *Not today.* I didn't want visitors. The knock continued and Ben popped his head in saying it was Isabella, and she was very adamant about seeing me, and she would wait for me to get up. Good thing I was still under my covers and Ben couldn't see the shock across my face. What would Isabella want with me? Didn't she already have enough fun with her cousins last night? I wanted to say no, thank you, and send her on her way, but something told me Isabella was not used to hearing no and was quite stubborn as well. I stuck a hand out of my covers and waved to Ben and flashed five fingers at him twice. The door closed so I guess that worked. Then I realized I just didn't care. I was the owner of this place and she could flaunt herself and get her way everywhere else but here. With that said, part of me still wanted to show her I could also look great. So I got up, picked out my favorite dress that accentuated my figure, and put earrings in. Then I didn't know what else to do. But at least I wasn't in jeans and a t-shirt. I took a deep breath and walked out of my room to greet the last person I wanted to see after the events from the previous evening.

"Isabella, what a pleasant surprise. Is there something I can help you with? Did you forget something last night? You could have just called. I would have been glad to mail it to you," I said in a rush, knowing full well I should have stopped after question number one.

She looked me over and took a deep sigh before she put on a fake smile. She, of course, was dressed immaculately. Designer white fitted business dress that was cut right above her knees and accentuated all her curves, covering the shoulders just to show the right amount of skin and the beautiful long arms that ended in perfectly French manicured nails. Her face displayed just the right amount of makeup to show that she wasn't at an evening event, but was paying a nice visit to an acquaintance, and her hair was done up loosely to give the feeling of "Oh, this hairdo? I just put it up with a hairband and that was it." Beautiful three-inch heels made her legs look long and taut. I felt like a frump next to her. At least I put earrings in.

"Merry Christmas. I came specifically to see you," she said, "Anne, we've gotten off on the wrong foot. I came to apologize for my cousins last night. They were way out of line." This whole time she was looking around the foyer. She had the kindest look when her eyes settled back on me.

"I really hope I can make it up to you! I've always wanted to see this house more. We used to come when I was a child, but I haven't visited in many years. I was wondering if you'd be willing to give me a tour. I have a degree in interior design and could help you update the look of the place. I can only imagine my great-uncle being old-school and keeping things the way they were when he was a little boy. My mom has always said he loved to live in the past," she added.

"Oh, well come in. Would you like a drink or a snack?" At least I didn't forget my manners.

"That won't be necessary. I have a 10 o'clock appointment, so I can only stay a little while, and I want to get the most out of our visit."

Isabella spent a long time looking at the carvings in the walls in the foyer, the staircase, the paint color, the trims, the molding, and the door carvings. She hummed and hawed over every detail making me nervous as I walked behind her and tried to supply answers where I could. I had Andy follow us as he could provide more details than I. I learned a lot such as Sir Anthony started a lot of his carving work in his early twenties and started carving in the house in his late twenties right up to his passing. From the sound of it, he covered the house in them and got pretty proficient. But some were so small that I had missed them. We found blossoms on almost every item. Either one big one or many small ones off the branches. Some carved into the wood, some painted a soft pink. We spent so much time in the foyer that I started seeing them everywhere. In nooks and crannies. Even some ornate tables in the entryway had not been safe from his scalpel. Isabella wanted to get rid of it all.

"These carvings are a monstrosity and out of place in a grand house like this. If I was Sir Anthony's wife, I would never have let him do this to such a gorgeous house. Did you know that this house was built by my great-great-grandfather? He hired the best architect of his time. It took my great-great-grandfather a whole year just to get on his calendar and even then, he had to wait another year before the house was started. And now look at it. Carved up as if it was driftwood he found on a beach. It does you such a disservice as you are trying to make a statement with the new crowd you will be spending time with. My suggestion would be to cover them up with sheetrock and make everything smooth. A fresh coat of paint and some expensive well-known artwork will modernize the place and really make everything shine."

"I could use some of my mom's artwork." This made her pause, but only for a second.

"We will of course also change the lighting. There are so many dark spots in the ceiling and around the turns of the hallway. You could really make the place light and airy with just the right light fixture. And we must change everything to LEDs. They are the latest craze and would save you money in the long run. Not that that is a concern of yours anymore, but it'll make you sound educated."

At first, I was a bit disgusted by all her assumptions. I could see the love that Sir Anthony put into his work, and I thought it made the place feel more like a home. But then my thoughts went back to last night and meeting all the rich family and friends of Sir Anthony. Many were pleasant, and I would like to get to know them better. Maybe it would be a good idea to bring the house up to a modern standard, or at least something closer to my taste. Before I could even inject a word, she was already onto the biggest object in the foyer.

"Now for the chandelier. I was told that it was to resemble a plum blossom tree in the spring when all the flowers had just bloomed, but do you really see it? It's just a bunch of diamonds put together in a big random mess and hung up to dazzle. Now I'm all for the diamonds and the dazzle, but I think you would do better with repurposing the diamonds and incorporating them in jewelry, maybe as a gift to someone you know, or even a new chandelier," here she lingered on me for a split-second "or sell the diamonds to get new items for the house decor. I know a company that you could sell it to. They could re-purpose it or give you good money for it. Here, I wrote down their number on my card." I was getting a bit peeved by her constant barraging of everything I knew was probably very dear to Sir Anthony and maybe Ai Po, but I could also see her point. Plus, Andy would put his hand on my shoulder every once in a while to calm me down. So, I kept my mouth shut when necessary and waited to see how things went for the rest of the tour.

We went through all the main parts of the house with Isabella making comment after comment. By the end of the tour, I was exhausted. Isabella seemed to really want this relationship to work, both the renovation and getting to know me. She had been cordial all morning, and I had to admit I enjoyed the new company. I still didn't know if I could completely trust her, but I was warming up to her and starting to see the changes myself. I was getting excited about putting my touch on the house with Isabella's help. Maybe this would be a start for being accepted into this new world I had entered.

"Thank you so much for showing me around today. I have wanted to revisit and I'm so thankful you had the time to walk through the house with me. Why don't we meet up tomorrow and I'll bring a mood board to show you?" She was already dialing in her phone and walking out the door before I could respond. It was like a running dialogue that you had to chase after to hear the whole thing.

"Um, sure, tomorrow will work fine," I called after her. She turned to give me one of her maybe-fake-maybe-genuine smiles and drove off.

"Well, that was quite a whirlwind, wasn't it, Andy? I learned a lot, and it seemed Isabella is really trying to make it work. It was so nice to have someone new to hang out with even if it was more one-sided the whole time."

"Anne, if I may say . . ." Andy paused and seemed to be studying the marble floor looking for something he'd forgotten.

"What is it, Andy? I've never seen you be bashful when talking with me."

"I hate to talk bad about any of the Wilkens family behind their backs, but Isabella is not one to be trifled with. She can cause a lot of problems if you give her too much room. She thinks she means well, but has grown up always getting what she wants. For example, I could tell some of her suggestions really bothered you. You must speak up as it is your house. Let me ask you, do you feel that this is your home?"

"Of course I do. I live in it right?" I didn't mean to sound annoyed, but the more I thought about the question the more I got uneasy. Of course, I thought this was my home, didn't I?

"Yes, yes. I did not mean to offend. Just watch out for Isabella. She and Sebastian used to be a couple, and I remember Sebastian being very hurt."

"Thanks, Andy, I'll keep it in mind." Why did I feel jealous at the mention of Isabella and Sebastian being a couple? Maybe because she was gorgeous and had everything. I shook my head and pushed the thought aside. Really, what was there to worry about? I was assertive in everything in my life and I wasn't about to keep quiet about the remodeling of my home. Her surprise visit had flattered me, and I was looking forward to her mood board tomorrow.

Now, what was I going to do the rest of the day now that I was up? Lunch would not be a bad call and there was some food from the gala I did not get to try. I ventured toward the kitchen in hopes Cook saved the leftovers.

After a most delightful lunch, I ventured to the garden to have a walk around and see if I could see any carvings on the outside of the house. Maybe I'd also ask the stable boy if he'd teach me how to ride a horse. Owning a stable meant I needed to ride. At least that was the logic I put behind it. But as I turned the corner to head to the stable, *wham!* I ran smack into someone's chest.

"Well, hello, that's quite a greeting. Being almost knocked over by the very woman I came to see."

"Sebastian! What are you doing here?" I blushed all over, remembering our kiss from last night. My knees started wobbling, and I put a hand on the wall to steady myself.

"I told you I'd stop by to check on you today. Is that still okay?

And Merry Christmas." He was more jovial today than I had ever seen him. Smiling, hair tousled as if he had literally rolled out of bed and didn't do his usual grooming, wearing a t-shirt and jeans. Definitely not the Sebastian I was used to, but I liked it. I could feel myself slowly losing my senses and yet I couldn't look away.

"Do you want to come in?"

"Well, I was just talking to your stable boy. I know this is your favorite time of year, and I was wondering if you would like to go on a carriage ride with me tonight?"

"You got a carriage?"

"Actually, it's yours. You can be safe in knowing that you probably own one of everything you can think of somewhere in this world, and if you don't have one, you could probably buy it."

I looked at him, dazed, as that one sentence was something I never thought I would ever be associated with. "Yes, that would be lovely, but can we go see this carriage of mine?"

"Right this way, my lady," and as we walked toward the stable I could hear a stifled laughter from Sebastian. He looked so relaxed. I liked this new Sebastian.

Old with dust and debris all over it. You could see a faint red under the dust with white trim around the edges. With some cleaning and shining it would really look beautiful.

"Brent here has said he would start cleaning it and have it ready for us after dinner. Since your horses aren't here at the moment, he said your neighbor, Lindsay, would be glad to let us borrow hers for tonight. What do you think?"

"I love it! I can't wait!" I couldn't stop smiling. This was more than I could ask for. A romantic experience with the man I had growing feelings for.

As we walked back toward the house, I asked Sebastian about Isabella. He paused longer than I thought, and I was about to ask why when he said, "Isabella is quite an interesting character, and Andy might have a point in his warning, but I don't think you have anything to worry about. Isabella is harmless, and she really is one of the best interior decorators in the area. You can't go wrong with working with her. She loves this house and would want the best for it."

"Well, coming from you that is comforting." If he could say this about Isabella after being hurt by her maybe she wouldn't be bad to work with. "So, did you have anything planned or shall we just have a stroll through the garden? I'm not much in the mood for reading my grandmother's journals at this time."

"Actually, I do have plans. What do you think of surprises? It's my Christmas gift to you."

"As long as I'm not inheriting anything else for a while," which made him laugh his wonderful loud laugh.

First stop was an ice-skating rink. It was one of those mobile ice rinks they set up where they could find space. For Christmas day there were quite a number of people out. I immediately got tense as I was not a sporty person and definitely did not know how to ice-skate. But that was not a valid excuse, apparently. The next thing I knew I was donning skates, one hand holding the wall, and one hand holding Sebastian's. We walked slowly all around the rink three times and then he made me let go of the wall. He held my hands while he skated backward, never looking away from me, and I'm sure I was blushing up a storm. We then walked around the Pearl District and window-shopped, which was great fun as Sebastian made comedic comments about the window displays the whole time. Another trait I didn't know about.

"Here we have today's contestants. Window number one shows the latest in parkas. See how the length goes down past the knees and the latest technology has made it even thinner to where you don't have to look like a marshmallow in order to stay warm. Now in window number two, we have the mountain parka. It's the same as our magnificent choice in window number one, but with fur on the inside and the outside," and on and on he would go. I was laughing so hard I had to remember we were still in public.

He said he had wanted to treat me to a fancy dinner, but the only restaurant open was some Chinese restaurant in Old Chinatown. He seemed amazed by this, but I just laughed. Chinese restaurants were always open on Christmas, and I realized I had always taken that for granted. We were even treated to a couple special dishes. When the cook found out who I was he came to greet us personally. He knew Cook very well and had a high respect for her.

Sebastian surprised me more by pulling out a red journal no bigger than his hand with the creamiest paper inside. It was one of those lay-flat ones, and I couldn't wait to take my pen to it. He said he hoped I would have as much enjoyment in writing in it as my Ai Po had. I congratulated myself that I did not burst into tears at that moment, but I felt so special and cared for. It made me happy that we had both shared Ai Po's story and that he understood how much it meant to me.

Then, I had to go and ruin it all. The food was delicious, the company was fantastic, but I had to ask the question that had been on my mind.

"Sebastian, why do you like me?"

"Um, I feel like that's a loaded question," he said while swirling his wine glass.

"I'm not the type of person who attracts people, but all of a sudden I'm going out to dinner and having a grand time with a guy who many girls would fight over. The only thing that has changed in my life is that I'm now rich."

"I'm definitely not after your money," Sebastian replied while laughing. "If I wanted money, I would have married one of the many girls you say would fight over me."

"Am I the first non-white person you've dated?"

"Anne, what is this? We're having a great time together."

"It's just a feeling. I had an encounter with Isabella's cousins at the gala, and now this incident with my grandmother. It's bringing up memories of being teased at school, and believe it or not, it's something that I think of when I'm around white people."

"Which cousins are we talking about? And why would you worry about something like this? You're saying you notice that you look different from others?"

"Bernice, Kevin, and Jessica. They were super nasty and very racist in their remarks. I had never heard anything like it before. And yes, I notice when I look different from others."

"Oh, them! You can't take anything they say seriously. Those three are always looking for trouble and will rile anyone up to get attention. It's all a by-product of their grandmother, Geraldine."

"Just like that? I'm supposed to ignore everything they said?"

"I don't know what they said, but I wouldn't worry about it. You're overly sensitive. Isabella even came and apologized for their action."

"You don't get made fun of by your appearance and forget about it. You live with it, and every encounter makes you more aware of any staring, private talking, or sweeping aside of comments that people make because they think everything is 'okay.'"

"Whoa, I just want to have a nice night with you. Why don't we start over and let me take you on that sled ride? I can give you more kisses to make up for their rude comments." At this, I clammed up and got red in the face again. I was very flattered and starting to get confused with all my feelings. Brian had never taken me on a date like this before. He would take me to carnivals and eat hot dogs, which I loved and was right up my alley, but at some point, it would have been nice for him to have surprised me or . . . sigh . . . I needed to stop thinking about him. He was my first boyfriend and an awful one at that. I didn't want to ruin the rest of the night.

Sebastian brought me home, and we went on a sled ride right in my very own backyard. The rest of the night was awkward, but I couldn't have asked for a better ending. When we got back to the house, he pulled me in for a tight embrace and the best and longest kiss I had ever had. He slowly let me go and bid me goodnight. I must have stood at the entrance for some time just staring down the drive watching the tracks disappear between the trees. It was a night I would never forget, but there was much to think about. I had never had anyone treat me this well, and it felt really nice. To have someone who enjoyed my company. Now I knew how Victoria felt with boys ogling her all the time. It's nice to be wanted, but it still made me nervous. What if this was all a facade, and I got hurt again? I didn't have anyone to talk to about it either. Victoria had called saying her flight had been canceled and she couldn't leave until tomorrow. She had spent so much time on her phone making changes, it had died before she could get a hold of me. Then she had to make all the changes for her connecting buses, planes, and trains. She was on her way, she promised. Mom had left last night exhausted and had said she needed a couple of days to herself, which meant about a week. I laid in bed replaying the night with Sebastian and running through conversations from acquaintances that said mixed relationships just didn't work. There was too much of a cultural difference. Then, I also had acquaintances who had been in mixed marriages since it became legal in 1967, and they thrived through the ages. Brian was safe. He understood the Chinese side of me, such as I had never used a dishwasher before until Cook admonished me for washing dishes by hand. Dishwashers were always used for storage. I took pictures of everything. I loved deep-fried stinky tofu and Chinese pop bands. I had jet black hair and looked 100% Chinese, which in itself brought a lot of expectations of family before the individual, perfect grades in all things academic, respect to all elders under any circumstance, and being successful to make your family proud. Thankfully, my mom was never extreme in pushing these ideals on me, but I still grew up in the Chinese culture. It was hard at times to know if I should listen to my Chinese culture or American culture. I finally fell asleep telling myself I was once again overthinking everything.

28

ISABELLA CAME JUST like she said she would, but this time with assistants loaded down with samples, binders, furniture, paneling, and boards filled with ideas. We spent a good part of the morning going through everything. There were mood boards that were beige and others with so much color it was like someone took the rainbow and whacked it on the board. Then she had ones where there was the perfect blend of wood, neutral, and splashes of pinks, blues, and greens. The artworks she was suggesting were beyond what my brain could even comprehend. Neither one of us brought up my mom's paintings again. I would bring them in myself. She said I needed expensive artwork to show my worth to others. These were artworks that her "minions" were standing by at auction to bid on, and worth hundreds of thousands each. We decided on five of them leaving me shell-shocked that I just spent a million dollars in ten minutes. The rest of the morning went about the same as Isabella was bent on getting as much done today as she could and didn't leave much room for me to catch my breath. The wood pieces were brought in to match the wood in the house so that they could pick exact paint colors to match. Sheetrock workers were scheduled to start work on covering up the carvings in a week. This is where I started getting anxious as my first thought was I hadn't even gotten to study the house in much detail. There was so much I still had to learn. Why were there so many carvings around the house and what had it meant to Sir Anthony? I thought the carvings were so beautiful. She could tell I was getting hesitant on the new design, but she talked me through each detail and it made sense. Isabella was the expert in this field and I respected experts. It would be nice to update the house, and I didn't want to offend. I didn't know the first thing about how to start, so I agreed to most of the designs and was very appreciative of everything she put together. Isabella left in the same whirlwind she came in on, and I was left staring at the fire in the library feeling unsure about the decisions we had made.

Luckily, Sebastian came by and distracted me. We went out and had a lot of fun swinging on the swings in the playground and having a picnic in the park. But I could tell our comfort level had gone down a notch. My nerves were on high alert with his full attention on me, and I was so aware of my Chineseness that I could tell I was not as laid back as before. My whole body was tense, forced laughter, and I couldn't look him in the eye most of the afternoon. He ended up dropping me off before dinner as I said Cook was making something special for me tonight. He said he needed to head home to take care of something and left giving me a kiss on the lips, which I half-heartedly returned. I could tell he was confused, and all I could think of was how I was so good at repelling guys and Sebastian wasn't immune to it. I consoled myself that night by telling myself he was not a good fit for me. He was everything I was not and would disrupt all my plans in life. Though what those plans were, I wasn't sure.

❀

The next day, I was looking forward to Isabella coming over so I could be distracted from thoughts of Sebastian. She had left yesterday saying she was going to redo the samples and come back with more details. Part of me was wondering how she put all of this together in such a short time, but she was the professional and I had enough on my mind. I pushed it aside and enjoyed digging through all the samples and images she had brought.

"Thank you so much for spending the time to do this," I said to Isabella halfway through our morning work.

"No problem. I'm so glad you let me help. It's not like I'm doing it for free," she looked at me and laughed as I was surprised for a split-second, but corrected myself as of course, she would charge. This was a huge project and no one would do it for free. "But you will definitely get the family discount. It's the least I can do to help out our new family member."

"That's very gracious of you. All your choices have been beautiful and really speak to me. You've been so open to my suggestions and I cannot wait to see the changes." Though I still felt apprehensive about covering up everything. Last night I had sat at the bottom of the stairs looking at all the carvings. Why put all this work into these? Was he trying to achieve something or was it just a hobby that had gone wild? I knew it was something to do with Ai Po as there were blossoms everywhere, but it couldn't possibly have been all for Ai Po. The house was covered in it. Beautifully done and elegant but still covered.

"Oh, I have to get this phone call. It's my mom. You know how moms are," she said with a smile and walked out of the library to take the call. I was glad for the break as we hadn't stopped even for a second since she came.

"Everything okay?" I asked as Isabella walked back into the library.

"Everything is great. It's going just as I planned." Isabella sat down and stared at me.

"What plan?"

"You really think you own this house, don't you?"

"Well, I did inherit the house and you and I have been spending . . ."

"Yeah, yeah, the stupid will. Great Uncle was not of a sound mind in his old age. I think Andy covered up all the problems he had because of appearance, but we as family knew better. There's no way he would have given the house to someone like you," Isabella said interrupting me. "Mom said Great Uncle went crazy after their seamstress left. The whore brainwashed him. She used her exotic skills to try to reap his fortune," she said as if this was an everyday statement.

"What? Isabella, I'm not sure what you're trying to say."

"I'll say it very slowly as English probably isn't your first language, You...Do...Not...Own...This...House. On paper, sure, but that will be taken care of soon."

I was getting really fired up now. "What in the world are you talking about? We've already picked through three-quarters of the design. We were going to go out tonight to celebrate the start of the renovation. I live here. This is my house!"

"Oh, sweet Anne, you are so naïve. All these mood boards I've been working on for weeks. I've been looking into you. Asking around to figure out what type of person you are. You're so much easier to figure out than many of the other people who have gotten in my way. You've made yourself quite comfortable since moving here. I can't blame you. If I had all the money in the world, I would also have someone cook for me every single day, make my bed for me, clean up after me, and not worry about a thing. Oh wait, I do have that," she laughed.

"I do not do that! I pull my weight around here. You can ask any of the staff." I don't know why I was even arguing with her. I usually kept my cool much better than this. There was something going on, though, and it was making me very uneasy.

"Whatever, it's too good of a life for you. This place needs a mistress who can hold up to the grandeur of the place. Someone who blends in to this society, if you know what I mean. Someone like me." I just stared at her. This wasn't the Isabella from the last two days, and before I could respond to her dissing my ethnicity, she threw another blow. "The phone call I was just on was with Sebastian."

"Sebastian? What does he have to do with this?! Whatever this is?!"

"Did you know Sebastian is the family lawyer? He always was, even when Sir Anthony was alive. I've gotten to know him quite well.

Probably better than you. Don't look so dumbstruck. I know all about you and Sebastian. Reading those stupid journals of your grand-mother, kissing under the blossom tree, going out on dates. You can't hide anything from me. Well, the other thing you probably don't know is that Sebastian just agreed to marry me." The gleam in her eyes seemed to intensify as she leaned closer to me. I had stopped breathing at this point. "Sebastian is mine," she seethed. "He always was. You're not the first girl he's gotten infatuated with and wandered off to play, but he always comes back to me. Sebastian does my bidding, and as we speak, he is figuring out a way to get around the will. There's always a way around. You will get nothing." Here, she paused as if to compose herself. "Well, look at the time, I must go. Thank you for picking out all the details for renovating this horrid looking place. Everything's already been charged to your account, and the schedule will start just like we said. My foreman will be in touch with you and . . . well, I guess that's it. You'll be hearing from my lawyer," she said as she collected her things and headed to the door.

As Isabella drove away, I let out a bloodcurdling scream. Why did I trust her? I knew she was a monster. I knew it, and yet I had still hoped I had read her wrong. What happened to trusting my intu-ition? It had always served me well in the past, but somehow this whole house had made me vulnerable. Or maybe it was Sebastian. Engaged! What the fuck? The bastard just kissed me yesterday and took me out for fun and dinner. I was falling for him. Engaged! Around and around I went pacing the library like a mad woman. I knew I was going to get hurt. I knew it! Out of the corners of my eyes, I could see Andy, Ben, and a couple other staff members peeking into the library with worried looks. I willed myself to calm down, but every breath brought a new heat of anger and I started to cry.

What had I done wrong? How did I get into this mess? I know how. I had opened myself up to new possibilities, a new life, and a boy I had just started getting to know. I had done all that and every-thing had come back to flatten me. Well, I wasn't going to sit back and let them take my new home. Especially, not after learning all about Ai

Po's life here. I was the rightful owner. Sir Anthony had explicitly given me the house. First thing, I was going to go hunt down Sebastian and figure out what the heck he was going to do about it. Two could play at this game.

As I walked out of the library I turned to Andy, "How lucid was Sir Anthony?"

"He was very lucid. He could recite everything he ate and stories from any time in his life."

"Good," and I walked up to my room to defuse before finding Sebastian.

❧ 29 ❧

STANDING in front of Sebastian's building, I was glad I bumped into Cook who made me eat something before heading out. She and everyone else I passed had worried looks on their faces. I don't know how much they had heard, but I wasn't going to let anyone make a fool of me.

I took in the immense sitting room outside his office. This was where it all started. Where my life changed completely and where I met him for the first time. How I wished I could turn back time and decline everything that was bequeathed to me. I took a deep breath and walked toward the secretary.

"Ms. Huang, we've been expecting you," she said without a single emotion showing on her face.

"Expecting me?" I stopped in my tracks for a second before recollecting my thoughts. "I need to see Sebastian."

"Yes, like I said, we've been expecting you. You may go in."

I was at a loss for words and she still didn't have an expression on her face. Then I had to remember she worked for a guy who was supposed to be very good at what he did, swindling people's emotions. When I walked in, Sebastian was sitting at his desk looking right at me. However, the Sebastian I expected was the cocky, sure of himself, well put together lawyer. But this Sebastian looked like he hadn't slept last night and had been put through a ringer. My heart pulled at him and I wanted to run over and give him a hug. The way he was looking at me made me think that he wouldn't have said no to it. But I had to remember that he was a sniveling, untrustworthy person.

"Hi, Anne." His voice was so distraught I almost broke down again, but my anger won over all of my emotions.

"Based on the way you look and that you expected me here, I'm assuming Isabella has talked to you. Would you care to elaborate on the situation?"

"Please, would you like to sit or have a drink?" He got up to walk to the bar.

"No, I want an answer from you."

"Well, I need one before I answer. Please sit, Anne. I think we can talk better if we both sit."

"Sebastian! I'm not here to have a conversation. I want to hear from you what is going on!"

"Okay, okay. You deserve to be caught up. Let me just sit." He slumped onto the sofa and let out a big sigh. "So, Isabella . . . Isabella has told you I am working on the reassignment of the house. You have to understand I'm stuck . . ."

"Stuck? Reassignment? Why would you even be looking into this in the first place?!"

"They want me to find a loophole. I didn't promise them anything, okay? But I am their lawyer. I'm under contract and I'm indebted to them. I grew up poor, and they sponsored me through college as well as gave me the job I have now. I've gotten to where I am because of them. You have to understand, Anne. They would make my life hell." The words just tumbled out of his mouth in one big jumble of multiple thoughts at once.

"That is the most selfish thing I've ever heard you say. What about marrying Isabella?"

"Marrying Isabella?"

"Don't act like you don't know. She said you two were engaged. I thought you felt differently about me. I thought there was some feeling behind those kisses we had!"

"There was! Anne, I . . . I never said I would marry Isabella. I talked to her yesterday, and she asked if I had made my decision to marry her, and I said I was still thinking about it, but . . . but . . ."

"Still thinking about it? That makes things so much better," I snarled.

Sebastian put his head in his hands and started shaking it back and forth. "Anne, I'm very confused."

There were no more words. I had no idea what I had hoped to accomplish. Sebastian looked like a mess, and our conversation was going nowhere. I was so mad.

"You are a miserable failure of a man. I hope I never see you again." I left the office with tears streaming down my face before I even reached the elevator. As the doors closed, I saw him standing at the entrance of his office looking at me before he closed the doors.

It was time for me to move on. Maybe I'd stay with Mom for a while, get my next round of travels sorted out, and be on my way. I drove to the house and stormed to my room while the staff just stared at me. I'm sure they were in turmoil again wondering where their jobs would be. I didn't want anything to do with being rich if this was what it was like. With my phone nearby, I threw stuff into suitcases while waiting on the line for my mom to pick up. What was I going to say to her? I just learned the boy I like is engaged to someone else, and that was the case before he even met me? That everything we had inherited was going away if Sir Anthony's family had anything to do with it? That I felt like a failure? I wasn't in the mood to listen to a lecture about how I should have heeded her advice about not digging too deep, but I didn't know where else to go. This was not my home. I don't know if it ever really was.

"Hi, Sweetheart, I'm about to go to a movie. Is this quick?" she answered on the third ring.

"Hi, Mom, would it be okay if I moved back in with you?"

"Of course you can! But how come? Move back, as in you're not going back to the house?"

"Some things have happened and I need to go somewhere else." There was silence at the other end of the line, and I could hear my mom's thoughts running through her mind coming up with a thousand reasons why I would move home at the drop of a hat. All the reasons being bad ones.

"I'll see you soon then." And with that, she hung up and I'm sure went to make up my room, which I couldn't wait to get back to.

I packed up everything, which wasn't much, and brought them down to the entrance.

"Leaving us already?" said Andy looking older than he ever did while I was here.

"Just for this little while. I need to get out of this house."

"I understand. As far as we are concerned, you own this house and to tell you the truth, we are all petrified of Isabella and her family. Her grandmother and mother weren't so pleasant to be around when they were young, and Jacqueline brought up Isabella to be the same. I'm sad to see you leave."

"I'll come back and visit while this whole thing is getting sorted out," knowing full well that I probably would not be returning. I hated seeing Andy sad. He had helped me so much and really made me feel comfortable here. "Oh, before I forget. Could Ben help me bring down my grandmother's chest? That, I am not leaving here for anyone to take."

"Yes, of course. I'll go take care of that right now, and I'll have the driver meet you out front."

"Thank you, Andy. I couldn't have lived here for as long as I did, had it not been for you."

I settled myself on the bench by the front door and just stared at the grand foyer in front of me. There was still so much to discover about this place. Questions that I wanted answers to, but I couldn't stay here. I needed familiar ground to fight from. This was still my money to spend, and blast them if they thought I was just going to sit back and let them take it all.

"Anne, your car is here," said Andy.

"Andy, can you find the best lawyer I can hire? Clearly, Sebastian is not an option for this household anymore."

"Yes, I'll get right on that." He seemed to stand a bit straighter and his wrinkles seemed to shrink back a bit as a slight smile spread across his face. A ray of hope bloomed in me just to see that slight smile. He knew I wasn't going to just let this go.

30

"WOULD you like some eggs this morning?" asked my mom trying her hardest not to make a big deal about me moving back in. If I wasn't so morbid I would think it funny and be flattered that she was trying so hard to keep it together.

"I'd love some eggs, Mom. Why don't you come and join me for breakfast? You did great on the food. There's enough here for four people."

"It's not every day that my daughter comes home to visit."

"It's good to be here again." It made me sad to think I could have avoided everything if I had just denied the inheritance, but then we'd probably be second-guessing ourselves and wondering what our lives would be like.

"How long do you plan on staying?"

"I was thinking for a while if you'll let me?"

"Of course, of course. Can I ask what this is all about? You just threw that big gala, and I did think it was quite impressive."

"You thought it was impressive?" I looked up at her and saw a smile on her face and signs of worry. I didn't want to see any worry at this moment, but I felt a bit happier knowing that my mom thought the gala was impressive. That was a high compliment from her.

"Yes, it's a lot of work to put something like that together and everyone seemed to have a great time and there wasn't a flaw, at least not noticeable."

"How would you know how much work it takes to put on a gala?" I asked meaning it as a joke.

"I happened to be an event planner for two years when I was in my twenties. It was an emergency job after college when I couldn't find anything else."

"You were an event planner? But you can't stand to manage big projects like that!"

"Like I said, it was an emergency. I needed money to pay my loans. My artistic side did help though. I remembered doing quite a lot of painting then and many of the patrons started buying my work. It's how I got my start."

"Do you have pictures of the artwork?"

"I do. I'll see if I can find them later."

"Let's look for them now! I want to see what kind of events you put on."

"One day, Sweetheart. Right now I'm worried about you. You seemed to love living at the house. What happened?"

"I don't want to talk about it right now. I thought I'd take today off to get settled back in, and then maybe tomorrow we can talk."

"Okay, I'm going to go out and meet with Abigail. You call if you need anything. I planned a little something just for us tonight since we never got to celebrate Christmas together."

"Oh wow, thanks, Mom." I almost teared up feeling loved, but I managed to hold it together.

Ai Po's trunk was sitting at the foot of my bed and maybe it was because I hadn't gotten enough sadness in my life, or it was just plain curiosity, but I wanted to read her journals. I opened the trunk and took out all the items. Back in the comforts of my own room where there were no servants that would come around, I felt safe to just let everything lie where I put them. I curled up in bed and opened the journal.

36年4月20日 (Sunday, April 20, 1947)

Hi . . . It has been about a month now. My father sent a letter again telling me to come home right now, but the thought of leaving the city where Anthony is paralyzes me. I pretended I never got the letter and went to seek whatever job I could get. There was little work in being a seamstress as ready-made clothes were growing rapidly. Desperation was setting in by my second week. The last of my earnings was fading, and I was really hungry. I went into a bakery to see if I could get a small slice of bread, and the lady was so nice she gave me a whole loaf. She had so many customers that day she asked if I could help her. I got all the bread I could eat that day. She has had her bakery there for generations, but she had no help. Her husband was killed in the war and what help she could get would leave after six months to something better. She said she could pay me only a little, but she could provide room and board, and all the bread I could eat. We got along well, and I wasn't going to say no to this opportunity. She always wore a patchwork apron that had all sorts of colors on it. Her hair was always tied up in a handkerchief and she moved fast. It was all I could do to keep up with her. Her name was Josephine. I like that name.

That's my mom's name! I almost jumped up to tell Mom and remembered she was out.

On the third week, Dad showed up. My heart sunk even lower at the sight of him. He looked like he hadn't been sleeping, and he had aged so much since we arrived in the US. I knew a lot of it was because of me, and I almost packed up my things to go home with him. He yelled at me, telling me I dishonored the family, I was a wretched daughter, I had no honor or respect for myself or for my family, and on and on.

At this point, I had become quite independent, and I saw how the Americans lived and could choose what they wanted to do with their lives. I was making money and taking care of myself. When he finally quieted down he really got a good look at me and was surprised at the sight. I was rounder with all the bread I had been eating, and I didn't look worse for wear. What earnings I had I handed over to him, and I showed him all the work I was doing here. I cried and told him I felt like a wretched daughter. If time-travel was real, I would not be the girl who got carried away with her independence and what might have been an infatuation. I felt every level of shame you could imagine and then some. If I could have dug a hole to hide even lower, I would have. How could I have ever done anything like this? I think, deep down, he was relieved that I wasn't going back. They would probably have to hide me in the workshop and be embarrassed for me the rest of our lives. No one would come to ask for my hand and they would be devastated. It was better for me to stay up here and all he had to say was I was taking care of myself, which I can just see the elders nodding their head going "Good, she needs to take care of matters after what she did." I never heard from my mom though Dad says she's lost a lot of weight in the last week.

36年5月10日 (Saturday, May 10, 1947)

Sorry, I've not been around. It has been an emotional roller coaster for the last few weeks. I started thinking about Anthony, and I can't get him out of my head. My life here has been routine and nothing exciting or abnormal is happening. I meet Josephine at 4:30 a.m. to finish prepping all the bread and pastries. The rest of the day I would help wherever I was needed; serving, baking, cashier, or going out and buying a last-minute ingredient. As the days became more routine, I started to remember the walks we had and how he would just sit with me in the garden on our private bench and talk about anything in the world. We'd discuss the family business, the dreams he had for himself about becoming an artist, and what he had done in the war. We would talk a lot about my culture and how different it was from his, which I liked to remind him that, to me, it was his that was different from mine, to which he would laugh his hardy laugh and give me a kiss. He would tell me that he loved that I was independent and had my own mind. I didn't tell him he was the one that had grown this independence. I was not scared to correct him or discuss hard topics with him. He said he could see me being my own boss one day and running my own shop. He never treated me like a servant and said I had made him more humble. I loved him and I still do. I admit it. Maybe if we lived in an era where people of different skin colors could be together as equals we would be accepted. But there was also the money difference. I was a working girl. No father of Lord Wilkens' stature would ever want their child with a working person. It was a lose-lose situation we had gotten ourselves into. Maybe this was the best thing that could have happened to us.

36年5月14日 (Wednesday, May 14, 1947)

I received a letter from him! A boy stopped me in the street this morning and said someone had told him to give me this letter. He ran off before I could ask anything about it. My curiosity got me and I opened it then because, well, who would give me anything in the middle of the street? Good thing I was alone! I have been glowing ever since. I walked as fast and as casually as I could back to my room. It was in a very simple white envelope and had my name on it in Chinese. No return address and a simple note saying he missed me. His life hasn't been the same since I left and his father has been hounding him more and more about taking over the family business. He wanted nothing to do with his family if he couldn't be with me. He wanted to stay in touch and wasn't sure how to keep sending me letters without the family noticing. He hoped I had gotten this one and would wait with a sad heart to see if I would respond. He had found a trustworthy soul who would drop the letters off wherever I thought would be safe as well as pick up mine. He had told the boy to find me in two days to ask if there was a return letter. He still wanted to stay connected! That sent my heart soaring, and I cried the rest of the day while working. I was thankful for my private spot because no one saw me reading the letter every five minutes or crying to myself with happiness. I was so thankful I hadn't left Portland, and I had a private address for him to send the letters to. Josephine could not have been a better boss or friend. I told God every night how thankful I was. Things could have gotten much worse.

36年5月30日 (Friday, May 30, 1947)

It's been working, and I can tell his happiness has increased as mine has, too. We tell each other about our days and come up with ideas on how we can see each other again. Oh, how I wish it will be soon. At the moment, he can't get away from his family as his father has eyes watching him all the time. Everywhere he goes one of the servants—always male—has to go with him. What makes it worse is he thinks his father gives them an extra monetary bonus if they catch him doing something he shouldn't, such as meeting up with me. The letters come twice a week and I send them back equally fast. I've also started cooking food for Josephine and me to eat during our lunch break instead of pastries or sandwiches. I can't stand cold-cut sandwiches or pastries every day. I need hot meals. Josephine absolutely loves it.

It sounded like Ai Po was picking up pretty well after her big kick in the behind. I could only wish I was as strong as she was and could just move on with my life, but of course, when I thought about it, I was doing what she did, which was to throw myself into my work and forget about everything else. In Ai Po's case, she at least had a man who seemed to still love her and knew it. There were a couple spots where it looked like sheets had been torn out of the journal as if she was so mad she couldn't control herself. Interesting though, on the next page there was a newspaper clipping of Sir Anthony and another lady who definitely was not Ai Po. It was very obvious the woman in the picture had a white complexion, light hair, with big American eyes. Her figure was also very pronounced in all the right areas whereas I knew Ai Po was small in those same areas. My mom and I both inherited those features. But the clipping looked like an engagement announcement, and it was!

36年6月17日 (Tuesday, June 17, 1947)

We just weren't meant for each other (big blurry spot probably from tears). I had started dreaming of us running off together, starting our own business, doing so well no one could fault us for what we did as we would be happy, and we would be together. But it's all a dream (big tear stain). I received the following clipping in his last letter.

Dear My Love,

I'm devastated (but how devastated can a man be when he has a woman like that by his side). My father confronted me this week and said that he had chosen a bride for me. No one is more surprised than I am. He said it was time to step up to my place in this family and start producing heirs. I tried to get out of the engagement, but it was already set by both of our parents and the wedding was already planned for next week. It would bring both families together and make their business even stronger. My father then surprised me more that I would be really happy with his choice as it was my childhood friend, Sally. Sally and I haven't talked to each other since middle school. We have nothing in common except that our families are rich. She does not even come close to your independence and different way of viewing the world. I miss you terribly. I hate the whole thing and I'm so sorry that this is happening. I didn't want you to find out from someone else (big tear stain that wiped out the rest of the entry.)

Yours Always,

Anthony

The tear stains made me stop. The emotional connection with the girl I was reading about just made my heart break. The fact that it was my own Ai Po made it worse. I felt a tightness in my chest as I thought of how sad Ai Po's life had become. Anthony seemed to have really loved her and it made me so mad that they could not be together. It made me appreciate more how lucky I was to live in this era where I could choose whoever I wanted to be with, not that I had focused on that very much, which made me think of Sebastian. My blood boiled just thinking of him, but maybe Ai Po was right. We just weren't meant for each other.

31

MOM CAME HOME laden with food from the grocery store and gossip to share from her friends. It was nice to see her happy. She prepped a big dinner for us and I even got to help some. Cook had sent over her signature carrot cake, and I was excited to dig in. It was still the best I had ever tasted. I watched Mom as she arranged all the food in bowls, plates, and in rows on the counter. Her prep work was always as pretty as the end result. We ate in silence for a bit.

"I'm going to see Victoria tomorrow."

"You haven't seen her since she left?"

"Yeah, she left right when I got the house. She was supposed to be at the gala, but she's been delayed till now, and then her parents insisted she spend a day with them seeing as how they haven't seen her yet either."

"I'm glad you two have each other." I could hear my heart thumping it was so silent. We both knew what I wanted to talk about, but neither wanted to bring it up. I finally broke the silence.

"Mom, I just finished reading most of Ai Po's journals. They're very eye-opening. I feel like I got to know her a little. Are you sure you don't want to read them?" Mom started eating slower and started picking at her food. It unnerved me to see her quiet and not have a right-out opinion, but maybe she was contemplating it. I knew she had a rough time growing up with her mom, but I always thought it was because they grew up in two different cultures that clashed. Now I knew it probably went deeper than that. I thought the journals would really help her see her mom in a new light.

"I've read them before."

"What?" There was an awkward silence and Mom wouldn't look me in the eyes.

"You heard me," she was irritated, and I didn't know why. "I've read them before."

"How could you have read them? I only just found them when I moved in."

"There is so much you don't know."

"Then tell me! How could you have read these before, why didn't you tell me, and I don't understand? Mom, what do you mean?"

"Let's wait for dessert. I know how much you like that carrot cake. I haven't been able to have a nice meal with you at home anymore so let us just enjoy this moment."

She was stalling big time, but Mom never held back. I would wait. We ended up in the living room after dinner, and she still wasn't looking me in the eyes. I started feeling bad that I had ruined the night she had planned for us. What was this all about?

"I was young. I needed a job. This man approached me, Andy."

"As in Andy, the butler who still works at the house?"

"Yes, the same. Please don't interrupt or I might not be able to tell you the whole story. He said they needed someone with my talent to come work. Andy had seen me in the park painting one day and thought I was very talented. At least that is what he told me when he persuaded me to go. My skills covered many styles of painting. They wanted Eastern paintings and portraits to be made of the master. I was flattered and didn't think twice about it. I was young . . . so young . . . After working there a bit I started helping Cook in the kitchen as well. She was making her infamous carrot cakes even then. I had forgotten how delicious they were. One day, and I don't know why that particular day, Sir Anthony brought out a trunk that was the same one you found. He went on to explain that this used to belong to my mother. As you can imagine, I was shocked and couldn't make heads or tails of it. The more he talked, the more I got offended that maybe this was all a prank. There was no way my mom would have worked at a place like this. She abhorred rich people and always made sure we stayed away from them. It also made me mad that if this was true, I was learning about this new discovery from Sir Anthony and not my own mother. I took the trunk into my room where I was also living in during my tenure there, and for days I wouldn't touch it. Then curiosity got the better of me, and I started reading her journals. That chest should have never been opened. I have so much hatred for the whole household. I confronted my mom, and of course, she was so mad. She forbid me to ever go back. We got in a huge fight. Long story short, I quit that job, returned the chest, as neither Mom nor I wanted it, and I moved away for a while. I met your dad while away and when I had you I wanted to be closer to my mom. I thought if I moved back she would forgive me, and we could start over. Your Ai Po had so much pride and we both hurt. I went back and apologized, but the damage was done. Mom didn't like that her past had been brought up, and that it was done behind her back. You only got to see her a couple times. She died soon after you turned three, I think because I broke what remained of her heart. I have never quite forgiven myself for giving her such a hard time about the decisions she made when she was seventeen. But living through hardships myself has put her life into a different perspective, and I wish I could take back the mean things I said to her. Then this inheritance came up, and Anne, I didn't want anything to do with it. Their family has done nothing but hurt ours for generations now, and we don't seem to be able to get away. But I also didn't want to tell you what to do. I always made a point raising you to have your own mind, and I didn't think it right to change that now. I also thought this would be your only chance to get to know your Ai Po some. She is not as morbid as I've made her out to be. I should have prepared you more and told you this story at the beginning, but it was just too much for me to handle. I'm sorry. The money is nice to have, too, and

I feel guilty for using it in my decision to see how things played out. I still don't know what happened to make you come back, but it must be something to do with that boy. It's always something to do with a boy when a woman comes running back to their mother. Now you know. You can be mad at me, but this is the truth, and I can't tell you anything else. Seeing as how I reacted so negatively to them telling me, they must have wanted you to find it and think it was a lost historical artifact. I'm sorry I didn't tell you earlier, but it just brought back too many bad memories. Memories that I've been running away from ever since. You are the best thing that happened to me and I'm sorry I hurt you. That was not my intention, but I didn't know what to do. Now you know."

I sat there for the longest time not knowing what to say. She knew so much already and left me to fend for myself. Part of me was glad she trusted me that much to make my own decisions, but she knew. She knew and didn't tell me, didn't warn me, didn't provide any support. I got up, walked into my room, and shut the door. I needed to be by myself for the rest of the night.

32

I HUGGED Victoria for so long and she did likewise. She could not have come back at a better time.

"You want to tell me what has been going on? You look like you're about to cry. I'd like to think you missed me so much, but I haven't been gone that long, and we've been apart longer than this," she said, forcing me to let go, and placing me in my seat. "How is the rich life going?"

"Rich life sucks."

"Okay . . . you were so excited for the gala though. I'm sorry I missed it. I was so looking forward to people-watching with you."

"It would have turned out so much better if you had been there."

"Well, I wasn't, so catch me up, or do we have to sit here all day because I will."

"I think I'm on the cusp of losing the whole house. A niece of Sir Anthony threatened me the other day and I couldn't handle it. I came back to live with my mom."

"I was going to ask why you were back. I was expecting to meet you at the house."

"Well, at this point you might not see it for a while, if ever. I plan on fighting whatever is thrown at me, but I don't know what's going to happen at the moment. I confronted Sebastian the other day, and he said they've asked him to look into any loopholes in order to get the house back for them."

"Sebastian? You mean the hunk who you had a big ol' crush on?"

"I did not have a big ol' crush on him! Well, I guess we've gone on a couple of dates now. Yes, the one and the same."

"Dates?! You've gone on dates and not told me! And I thought he was your lawyer?"

"He is, but he is also the lawyer for the whole family and apparently they have made him who he is, and he's obliged to be faithful to them."

"And the dates?"

"Is that all you can concentrate on? My life is in tethers here."

"Okay, okay, please continue."

"Well, I was wondering amongst all your nefarious friends if there was a lawyer I could hire?"

"Ha, I'll ask around. Seems money won't be an issue so we'll find a good one for you. But what is going on with you and Sebastian?"

"You and your one-track mind. There were two dates, and I loved both of them. I have to admit I started getting cold feet because I'd never felt that way before. He is such a good kisser, he makes my whole body shiver, and I'm myself around him, but he's white and I'm Chinese and if you had read my grandmother's journals you'd understand all the racism she went through. It makes me nervous."

"You do know it's 2010, right? We've seen mixed couples growing up."

"Yes, yes, I know, but it doesn't mean everyone is happy now with all different colors of the skin. Anyway, now he's engaged to Isabella even though he says he didn't promise her yet. And I have found out more about my Grandmother than I probably ever wanted. And on that matter, I've also found out secrets that my mom has been holding in my whole life."

"Oh . . . my . . . god . . . I should never have left. This is all much juicer than anything I did or saw in Europe. Please, tell me more." I spent the rest of the morning catching her up on everything that had been going on.

Back at home, I found a brown envelope sitting at the foot of our door. It looked like a courier service addressed from Schuster and Schuster Law Firm. What ended up being a relaxed morning turned into a fireball inside me just seeing the name on the envelope. I picked it up by the corner as if it was going to bite me and went into the house. What I read made me boil and scream.

Plaintiff's Claim and Order to Go to Small Claims Court. A bunch of legal words, a date, and a time followed. What really boiled me up was the handwritten letter from Isabella. Even her handwriting was perfection.

Anne - you are hereby notified that we, the Wilkens Family, are suing you for emotional damage. All the hurt caused over three generations that has financially and emotionally stunted heirs from receiving what's rightfully theirs. Sweetheart, stay away from Sebastian, and enjoy what you can while it lasts. Your family has meddled in our family for too long, and I won't allow it anymore. I will protect my family and what's rightfully ours.
~Isabella

I screamed and slammed the papers down on the counter and crumpled them in my hand.

"What happened, Anne? Why are you so mad? What is that in your hand? What has been going on? I could hear you coming up the stairs. How many times do I need to tell you we have neighbors, and we need to keep our voices down?" Of course, Mom would walk in right then.

She took the papers while I walked into my room and slammed the door. I threw myself onto the bed hoping it would suffocate me and make all of this go away. But that was not to last, as next thing I knew, Mom was sitting next to me rubbing my back. I turned with tears in my eyes and she picked me up and held me. I couldn't remember the last time I cried in my mother's arms.

Sure enough, Victoria was still there when I went back to the café, but she waved me off. She was chatting up the same boy I had left her with inside in a private corner. I went out and sat at our corner and people-watched. How carefree everyone was. What I wouldn't give to only have my work to worry about.

"Can I join you?" I looked up to see a forlorn-looking Sebastian looking down at me. He was the last person I wanted to see, but he sat down before I could say anything more.

"I have something to confess," he said without looking at me. I tried to stop him to make him go away, but he raised his hand to stop me. I figured it wouldn't hurt to just let him talk. I didn't have to listen. My attention went back to the people on the street, and I wondered why Victoria hadn't come out.

"I'm assuming you got the subpoena? I'm sure you did by the way you're looking at me. Yes, I had to send it. You have to understand how hard it is to work for this family. They will ruin me if I don't do my job. They are my primary client and have given me all I know, and this is so not how I wanted this conversation to go. I really came to see how you are."

"How I am? How do you think I am, Sebastian? How?"

But he kept going on with his story as if he hadn't heard a word. "I found one loophole, Anne. Only one, and it was a slip from me and has been eating me up inside since I found it. Sir Anthony wanted me to change the will to include you, and in my rush to get it updated, I forgot to make a change he had insisted on. I really thought I had done it." I looked at him expecting more, but he seemed lost in his own thought.

"I forgot to make the change, which was to take Geraldine off the list of people who benefited from the will. I was supposed to have taken her whole family out. The house would go into the family trust if anything was to happen to you, which is run by Sir Anthony's siblings, including Geraldine. It doesn't help that Bernice and Catherine are nonchalant about the whole thing. They couldn't be bothered and have given all their voting rights to Geraldine. Jack is the only one trying to persuade her to drop the whole thing, but he's been unsuccessful. She's called him an—and please forgive me—Orient-lover just like their brother."

"Why are you telling me this, Sebastian? You said it yourself, your loyalty goes to that family and you can't do anything about it. So, move on, and I'll see you guys in court."

"I'm telling you this because I love you." At this, my head snapped back to look at him. I didn't know what to say and just stared.

"I've loved you for a long time. Sir Anthony asked me to follow you for the last five years and see what type of person you were. I had a good source that said you were from a reputable family even if socially and financially you were not up to the Wilkens family level. I even asked you for directions one day, and you didn't even know it. Then Sir Anthony said you were to inherit half the money and the house, and I am guilty of thinking that you were eligible now. Then, when you did inherit the house, I got to know you and Anne, I love you. But you seemed to want to distance yourself from me the last time we hung out and I got confused. Isabella has been asking me to marry her for a long time, but I don't love Isabella."

I looked at him in horror for I don't know how long. "The fact that you've followed me for five years creeps the living daylights out of me. But you love the money and status. You love being wanted and being something in people's eyes. Especially those who have influences you can use. You're nothing but a rat. Someone who feeds on others and goes from opportunity to opportunity. I never want you near me again. Go away, Sebastian." I got up to leave, but Sebastian grabbed my hand before I could walk away.

"Anne, please. They will stop at nothing to ruin you and your mom and will drag this lawsuit out for as long as they want. Just agree to their terms and let it all go. They have copies of part of your grand-mother's journals. Sir Anthony was notorious for being too trust-worthy and let people in and out of his house as they wished. I didn't know they had copies until they showed them to me yesterday. It's not worth it Anne. Please, I don't want to see you get hurt."

"Ha! Hurt? That's really what you're worried about? That's too late, Sebastian. I've never felt this level of hurt ever, and if you think I'm going to back down when someone's bullying me you don't know me at all. I will fight them until all they get is a shell of a house and no cash in the bank, and then they can have what they want."

"If this is any condolence, I'm no longer marrying Isabella. I told her a definite no today."

"That should never have been on the table, to begin with. I don't like being led on only to find out I was one of two in the race."

"Is something wrong?" Of course, Victoria would come at this time.

"I was just leaving."

"Oh! The infamous Sebastian. You look like crap, you know," said Victoria. "You're atrocious and have treated my friend like shit. I hope you rot in hell," she said. She hooked my arm, and we walked away with our heads held high. Sometimes I loved Victoria like the sister I never had.

✺ 33 ✺

AGAIN, someone had leaked to the local newspaper that I was a disgrace to the family and would not be having the inheritance for much longer. Walking down the street, I would get dirty looks left and right from total strangers. It's a wonder that some people believe everything they read as if they understood the situation just because of one article. In the meantime, I needed to see if my passport was updated and start figuring out how I was to get a visa to countries I wanted to visit. I also spent a lot of time at the library learning as much lawyer jargon as I could. Tangible things to do were good for me right now as every time I thought of the lawsuit I started boiling and couldn't let go.

"Have you had dinner yet? I've made your favorite green onion cookies."

"Thanks, Mom, I'd love some." Her green onion cookies always turned out so much better than mine and I still couldn't figure out why. "I'm thinking of heading to Taiwan, Hong Kong, Tokyo, Seoul, and then head down to Thailand, Indonesia, and we'll see where I go from there. Do you want to join?"

"This sounds like a much longer trip than normal."

"It's not like I will be gone forever. Just for a year or so. And you can come visit, too."

"We'll see." At least she didn't say an outright no this time. That was a win. I needed all I could get at this point.

"Thanks for the food, Mom. I'm going to head to bed. It's been a really long day."

"I love you, Anne."

"I love you, too."

I noticed Ai Po's journal still sitting on my nightstand. I cozied into my blankets and opened to the tear stains.

36年6月20日 (Friday, June 20, 1947)

A short letter today came when I wasn't expecting anymore. I had finally made up my mind that I was done with him this morning when I received this letter covered in blossoms as if he had stayed up all night just drawing all over the envelope. Inside was a very simple note asking me to marry him! He said he got to talk to Sally right after he sent the last letter, and she didn't want to get married to him either. He just told his parents that he wasn't getting married to Sally and that he was not going to take over the company. He was going to find me and marry me whether they approved or not. I was mixed with extreme joy and immense dread all at the same time. I could just see his father storming in with police and sending me off somewhere. But I was so happy that he loved me. So much so, he was willing to stand up to his father. That meant more than anything else combined. His letter didn't state more but said he would come to find me this weekend, and for me to pack and be ready. I was even happier because Mom sent me a letter saying she still saw me as her daughter and that she hoped I had learned my lesson. She explicitly said not to come home as my physically being there would cause more problems. I really hurt my family, but the boy I love is going to make it all okay. We're going to get married, and everything will be okay.

36年6月24日 (Tuesday, June 24, 1947)

I'm a stupid, stupid, stupid girl. I should have heeded what my mom wrote and really thought about the lesson I learned. Anthony came on Saturday just like he said. He was just as handsome as I remembered, and we kissed, hugged, and enjoyed each other all night. I showed him everything I packed and then realized he had brought nothing with him. I still held hope and thought he might have already brought his stuff to a hotel and had only come to pick me up. But as we talked, I realized something wasn't right. Eventually, the whole truth came out. His parents had taken his message of not marrying silently. He said his father had just sat there without an expression on his face. He took it as a sign that his father was just going to let things be, but he should have known better. While he was packing last night, he was brought into the library where two police officers were waiting. His father had told him that marrying a different race was against the law, and he would have his own son arrested—as well as me—and not think anything of it. He would also have me deported and all of my family as well. My family had looked into getting US citizenship here, but we quickly learned we were not allowed to. So deportation was a real thing. The consolation was that Anthony would still come see me this weekend, but it would be to end this "silly" relationship. "He had his fun with someone exotic" as his father put it, and it was now time to think of his future. As for Sally, Lord Wilkens and Sally's father had come to an agreement that their children would still marry next week. I could be with Anthony only if I was white and rich. Deep down, though, as much hurt as I was in, I felt for them as they were being forced into something they didn't want either. Life is so unfair. Anthony didn't leave until Monday morning. Josephine was kind enough to give us space and didn't ask me any questions, at least not till he left. I haven't stopped crying.

36年6月27日 (Friday, June 27, 1947)

Josephine wants to open a cafe in addition to her bakery. The spot next door is going up for rent, and she wants to rent it and have me run it. She says my food is good enough that it would sell itself.

The idea scares the living daylights out of me, but I have to keep myself busy or I will go crazy, and part of me thinks this is my chance. Therefore, I've been studying up on how to run a business and throwing myself into this new project. I miss him every day and I don't think my heart will ever heal. I've never been one to laugh or smile all the time like I see the Americans do here, so I just go on with my work. I got a letter from him today going back to our usual day-to-day stuff we do, but I only looked at it halfheartedly.

I was a great balled-up mess by this time. Mom had even peeked in because I was crying so hard. When she saw I was reading Ai Po's journals, she quickly left.

36年7月15日 (Tuesday, July 15, 1947)

I received a couple more letters from him and some drawings, but I haven't replied to them. I told Josephine everything, and she has been watching me like a hawk. Making sure I eat, bathe, sleep, and not write a letter to Anthony—basically keeping me alive. Even so, I've lost ten pounds already. I've had to use pins to keep my clothes on me. I would be happy to just melt into the earth. No one would miss me and Anthony would know I was gone, and he could focus on his new life and move on. But Josephine wakes me up every morning and gives me task after task to do all day long. I don't know what I would do without her.

34

I MUST HAVE FALLEN asleep reading last night because the journal was sprawled on the bed next to me with some of my drool on it. It had fallen open on a page with drawings. Each page had a drawing glued to it. They looked like the house, but the only difference was there was a man who looked like Anthony and a woman who looked like Ai Po sitting on the front porch, holding hands, and smiling. Another drawing had them in front of a cottage that had beautiful flowers in the front yard. They were standing in front of the house. Ai Po had a baby in her arms and Sir Anthony had his arm around both of them. Then, another drawing had them dancing under the moonlight on the sand with no one around. Just the two of them while they leaned against each other. On the back was always a blossom and "I miss you." There were more, and I assumed these were the drawings Anthony had done. Ai Po wasn't kidding when she said he was very talented.

I slithered out of bed and somehow got myself fed, dressed, and out the door. Taped to the back of the door was a note from Mom, "I had to go run an errand. I'll stop by the library today and we can have lunch. Love you, Mom." At least someone loved me unconditionally. I took the note and put it in my purse. It would give me the inspiration to keep moving through the day.

Walking to the library was no better today. Sideways looks and people turning their gaze when I turned to look at them. Lunch with Mom was really nice. She took me to a local Chinese restaurant. One that I grew up eating at, but for some reason, was exceptionally good today. We ordered more than we could eat and I brought the rest to the library to eat for dinner knowing I'd be staying late again.

"Anne, I love you. Don't come home too late, okay?"

"Thanks, Mom. I love you, too. I'll try. I really want to learn as much as I can, so I'm prepared for what's coming."

"Anne . . ."

"Mom, I'm fine. Please don't bring up Sebastian again."

"It's for the best, you know. You guys might have grown up in the same country, but you still grew up with different cultures."

"Mom, I know. He's out of the picture so there's no concern. Please stop bringing him up. He's a big part of the reason this whole mess is going on in the first place."

"Okay . . ." Mom wanted to keep talking to me, but she also knew I had shut myself off from everyone and everything. I was really good at doing that. She left, and I went back to researching, learning, and banging my head against the wall. The librarian eventually made me leave, but I wasn't ready to go home. The last book I was reading was about Taiwan, and I wanted to learn more. There was a café that I knew was open on the other side of town. And they had cheesecake if I remembered right. Some sweet dessert would be perfect right now. Maybe that bubble tea place would still be open, too. It wasn't that late, was it? Deep in my thoughts, I headed toward the garage. I thought I heard shuffling behind me as I got closer to my car, but no one was there when I turned to look. I remembered seeing a flash and feeling extreme heat. But the last thing I remember was something hitting my head.

I WOKE up with one arm and one leg in a cast, ribs that ached when I breathed, and beeping sounds all around me that made my heart rate start escalating before I could register where I was. Before I knew it, a nurse ran in and started pushing buttons around me and checking my body, but then I noticed the man standing behind her was Sebastian. He looked like he'd been sleeping on a sofa for days as his suit was wrinkled and his hair was a mess. His face had worry written all over it and he didn't take his eyes off of me.

"Well, it's nice to see you awake, Anne. Do you know where you are?" asked the nurse.

"It looks like a hospital room."

"Good, do you know what happened to you?"

"No, I remember being lifted off the ground and I hit something hard."

"Good. I'm going to go get the doctor. This young man has been here the whole time, so I'll let you two catch up." She left without any fanfare and my focus returned to Sebastian who had found a seat and was holding my hand in his two big hands.

"You've been here the whole time? How long have I been out?"

"Three days. Three agonizing days. I'm so sorry, Anne. If I had known . . ."

"Known what? What happened? Why am I all bandaged up?"

"Someone put a bomb under your car. It was detonated from a remote device so the police are assuming the person watched you until you were close enough. The blast would have killed you except you somehow ended up behind a pillar which took a lot of the blast. That's what you hit your head on."

"Why would anyone try to kill me?" I would have screamed if my chest wasn't burning every time I breathed.

"I have a theory, but it's only a theory."

"And that would be? What do you know, Sebastian? Did you have a part in this?"

"No! I didn't have anything to do with the bomb, but we have suspicions about who did and I wouldn't have believed they were capable of this. I know they're prejudiced to people unlike them, but I would never have fathomed they were capable of killing."

"Who, Sebastian? Be more specific."

"Nothing for you to worry about right now. I'm so glad you're awake."

"Who, Sebastian?" I asked in exasperation. I needed to hear it from him.

"Isabella and her family. Are you happy now?" He stood up with arms raised. He turned to look out the window.

"I needed to hear you say it." He turned to give me a glare. "So what does this mean now?"

"For what?"

"For what? For the house, for my inheritance, for the staff at the house?"

"I've been by your side this whole time! You want to talk about that now? You almost died! I almost lost you!" By this time Sebastian was rubbing his hair and looking at me like I had grown two ears on the top of my head.

"I'm awake, yes, I want to talk about this now. You haven't exactly been by my side before, and now that I almost died I want to be caught up."

"Well, I'm on your side now. I made a big mistake, and I'm truly sorry. I know you probably won't take me back, but I will fight for your side. The short answer is if you passed away the house would automatically go into the trust, which as I mentioned before, Geraldine holds 75 percent of the vote. When we prove that her family did this to you, then it'll be like no lawsuit was ever made by them. It'll just all go away."

"People like Isabella and her mom don't just go away. You of all people should know that. By the way, where's my mom?" All this back and forth was starting to wear me out, and the nurse had popped her head in to shush us.

"She's getting dinner together. She cooks up a meal every night in hopes you wake up so that you can eat decent food and not the garbage she says the hospital makes. I told her I would be here the whole time, so she's been at home cooking."

I didn't forgive him, but I liked having him here. They released me a couple weeks later, but I had to check in every week. At least I was able to sleep in my own bed. Sebastian was by my side the entire two weeks. He did some work from my hospital room, but he said his work could wait. I kept expecting him to change and disappear, but he was there tending to me the whole time. My mom made all my favorite foods, green onion cookies, sticky rice, and tomato with eggs. She invited her friends, and I had a great time singing, eating, and laughing with all the people I had grown up with. Victoria was there, and Sebastian stood off to the side the whole time, but he was there. I hadn't been this happy in a long time.

Mom and I ended up on the couch flipping through pictures of my young self. "You were so happy and confident growing up. So focused on your studies. I should have pushed you more to socialize with your peers, but I think you turned out alright."

"Well, thanks, Mom." I laughed and punched her in the arm. "I think I turned out just fine."

"I agree." She pulled me closer. She held me as we both cried. "Sweetheart, I have something for you."

"What is it, Mom?"

"You've been reading all those journals from your Ai Po, and we didn't exactly end on a good note the last time we talked about them."

"Not exactly, but if you don't want me to keep reading then I won't."

"No, no." *Thank goodness, because I was going to continue reading them.* "I saw the one you had finished reading. The one you left on your bed. I didn't want you to miss out on other parts of your Ai Po's story." She pulled a journal off the bookshelf and handed it to me. "This was one I kept. It's the start of her new life. Of when I came into the picture."

"Oh, Mom. This is wonderful. I'm going to read it right now."

"Maybe not right now. You need rest."

"You really think I can rest with this in my hands?"

"You're right," Mom said, patting me on my leg.

"Goodnight, Mom. I love you," giving her a kiss.

"Love you, Anne. Enjoy."

I went into my room and opened up the journal. I had to remind myself that Ai Po had a life after the house. And now that I thought about it, she wasn't at the house all that long and she lived to be 57. To this point I knew she was my Ai Po, but I hadn't really tied her to Mom or me. She was this third-party entity that somehow was related to us. I started to get nervous about opening the journal, but of course, my curiosity won.

36年8月1日 (Friday, August 1, 1947)

Good morning, here's to a new life. I am going to start my life over and try to move on. My parents are cordial to me, but it's just not the same anymore. They still haven't forgiven me for what I did. Many of the women have gone into factories to continue the work they did in the war. Since I'm not white, I'm not welcome in those areas and it is fine with me. Josephine needs me here, and I'd rather be cooking. I finally overcame my fear, and I went ahead with the café, and it's been rocky but good. People are open to the exotic food, and the Chinese people who are here are happy to have some familiar food as well, though everything is with a Western twist. Josephine has been ecstatic, though, I don't know how she can be happy all the time. I don't know if I'll ever be happy again, but I guess time will tell. I have to be strong and move on with my life. Plus someone has to do the cooking for this town. So many restaurants are understaffed. I can help by providing some cooking varieties in terms of food. Plus I still love the baking. I got one more letter from him right after the wedding, but none since. The wedding was small since neither one of them cared about it. I wrote back once, but it just didn't seem right anymore. He's a married man now. I will never forget him. He was my first love and will always be special to me. I can only hope that generations after me will have the benefit of being able to choose who they want to be with and not have social or racial boundaries. I just wanted to update you on where I was. I know I haven't written in a while and I probably will not be writing again for a while. There is just too much to do and there's no point in recording all my feelings anymore. I have new people in my life and a store to run. Food to make and people to feed. Oh, I almost forgot. The grocer's son came by yesterday. His name is Charlie, and he is from Taiwan as well. There are not many of us, and I stood out to him. He had been coming every day to buy bread from us, but I hadn't noticed him because I had sunk so low into myself. He asked me if I'd like to go to dinner one night, and before I could say no, Josephine answered for me and even told him when to pick me up. I think I gave her a glare. I hope I gave her a glare. He's cute, but I just don't want to be with boys anymore.

36年8月2日 (Saturday, August 2, 1947)

Okay, I enjoyed the date. He is handsome, kind, and patient with me. That's all I'm going to say.

36年9月1日 (Monday, September 1, 1947)

Don't judge me. Charlie has asked me to move to Astoria with him. He wants to try something new, and we can get a small house there, too. Josephine instantly agreed and is already making plans for me to open up my own shop there. I don't know how I got so lucky after what has happened. How could a person like me have met such good people as Josephine or Charlie? I don't know where I'd be now if not for them.

I wanted to keep reading, but I was so tired. Part of me was relieved that she had found some sort of peace or some sort of worth in her life. She was trying to move on, and she must have or I wouldn't be here in this world. Mom had mentioned before that her dad was called Charlie. Maybe I should give Sebastian another chance. He had shown that he really cared for me. He even sang tonight, which I had to laugh at he was so off-key, but his eyes were only on me, and he's slowly melting me. I drifted off to sleep knowing that things might be okay moving forward. Might be.

❧ 36 ❧

ANDY WAS EATING breakfast with my mom and I hobbled over and gave him a big hug.

"It's so good to see you," I said into his ear as he returned my hug.

"You hadn't visited in so long and we heard about your accident. I really hope it's not who Sebastian thinks it is, but I'm glad you are okay."

"What brings you here?"

"Can't I just come and see you?"

"No, you never leave the house. Ben is always the one who goes and does errands for you if it's outside of the house," I said while giving him a raised eyebrow.

"Ah, true. Nothing gets past you. Well, I also wanted to share some of my story with you."

"Are you going to tell me about the time when you were with my Ai Po?"

"No . . ."

"Still?!"

"Calm down. I don't need to tell you about the time I was with your Ai Po as you've already read her journals. According to your mom you've devoured them," he said with a chuckle.

"Then what are you going to share?"

"I want to share with you what happened after she got escorted from the house."

"Oh, but that was in her journals, too. I just finished reading those. My mom even gave me the journal where she starts a 'new life.'"

"A new life? Well, all of that was from her perspective. I want to share with you my story about what happened afterward. Let's go sit in the living room. I hope you two don't hate me more after sharing this."

"We don't hate you, Andy."

"You read that your Grandmother started a new life with her friend Josephine at a café. What you don't know is that I provided a lot of their income. It was post-war time, and they were struggling, though your grandmother probably would not admit to that. She was a very stubborn woman," he said, glancing at both of us. We smiled and nodded. We knew nothing about stubborn women.

"I had so much guilt inside me and I didn't want her to suffer more in life. Lord Anthony had started getting suspicious about the time Sir Anthony and your grandmother were spending together. He asked me to follow them around. Geraldine would sometimes see me spying and would tag along no matter how much I told her to get away. She was only ten at the time and wouldn't listen to anyone. She had her father wrapped up completely in her hands so everyone was terrified of her as well. I had to report everything I saw to Lord Anthony. He got so mad at one point he stormed around the house for days. Everyone was petrified that we were all going to get fired. You see, I was the one who told Lord Anthony and caused your grandmother to get kicked out." At this, he paused and tears started forming in his eyes. "I loved her, too, you know? But I was only fourteen at the time and I had nowhere else to go."

"His marriage to Sally was all a ploy to get him to forget Rose as well. He and Sally never loved each other. She knew there was this other woman, and they were such different people. He was devastated when your grandmother stopped sending letters back. After his father passed away, he had me find her and drive him to see her, but when we got there, he could tell she had moved on. He was heartbroken and I don't think he ever recovered. He loved her so much. The room you were staying in was the room your Grandmother had picked if she was to have a room upstairs. Sir Anthony remodeled it into a turret because she loved castles. He also commissioned the lady in the fountain to be your grandmother."

"I thought that looked like her! And the painting in the room?"

"Sir Anthony painted that himself. When I found out she had been pregnant, I felt even guiltier, and have never forgiven myself. I would order big meals from her café to feed the staff when Cook didn't have time to. It helped that I was the one in charge of making these orders so no one ever knew, though, I'm sure some had their suspicions. I would add on big tips and have the food delivered to a meeting point where the delivery boy would hand me the packages of food. I would send them red envelopes on holidays, and when she married, I sent over gifts to help them get started in their new life. Sebastian mentioned that he told you he had been following you for the last five years. I know it probably did not land on you well and I wanted to explain. Sir Anthony wanted to find you both to put you in his will. He disliked his family more and more as he grew older and wanted them to get something but so little that they would not be happy. Unbeknownst to him, I had never lost you two. I thought it would be suspicious if I kept sending you gifts once your grandmother passed away, but I never lost track of you. Sebastian had to make sure you were decent people and were nothing like Sir Anthony's family. I could tell after a few years that Sebastian had fallen in love with you. I never said a word as the boy had only his career and status in mind, but I could tell his heart thought otherwise. I want you to know that he means well. The boy is lost and has never had a good influence in his life except for Sir Anthony and me, which as you know, we are not normal people. Your mom said she shared with you the time she spent at the house. It backfired so badly that Sir Anthony did not include her in the will. He thought she would reject the whole thing and your mom has told me that was a wise decision on his part. We hoped you would be different, and I'm sorry your life was put in danger because of us. I'm so sorry for what I did, Josephine and Anne. I hope you two can forgive me."

We both gave Andy a hug. I know how much strength it took for him to come here and share all that with us.

"Andy, I want you to know that my mom had a good life. My father was a good man and her café was successful. She and Josephine ran it until they both passed away. She had a happy, fulfilled life," said my mom. I squeezed her hand knowing that she didn't talk about her mom easily.

"That brings me great relief and takes a huge burden off of my shoulders that I have carried for many years. I have something here for you as well. Sir Anthony wrote it when he was dying and asked me to hang on to it until the right time. I think now is the right time." Andy handed me a handwritten note that said:

Anne,

If you are reading this note, then you have read your Ai Po's journals. I hope that you do not judge your Ai Po too harshly. She was a lovely lady and I should never have shown her any interest. I should have known that she would never be accepted and my love would ruin her life. But I was in love with her and I still am. I wish, to this day, that I could have been married to your Ai Po and called you my very own granddaughter. I think of you as my granddaughter. Please forgive me (and Andy) as I believe he will have shared with you his story. He doesn't know that I know of all the good he has done for your Ai Po as well as the guilt he has carried for most of his life. I miss your Ai Po dearly every day and everything I have done with my life since has been with her in mind. My father was not a kind man, but he loved his family. I have no excuse for what he did and I can only blame it on the era he was born in. He had high hopes for me and did not want anything to get in my way. He ruled an empire, and he was hell-bent on keeping it. He confessed to me when he was dying that he made his decisions out of love. It was the only way he knew how to protect me from the rest of the family and to keep what he wanted, but in the end, he asked for my forgiveness. He never understood how I could love someone of non-white origin, but he wishes that he and I could have had a better relationship. Anne, I hope you are able to see both sides of our stories and you do not judge people as harshly as my father did. Love is not black and white. Be open to anything. I wish you much happiness.

P.S. I hope Sebastian gets his foot out of his mouth and asks you out. The boy is smitten with you. He is a good lad. A bit self-absorbed, but he will learn with time. I think that is something you can help with.

Much Love,

Anthony

❧ 37 ❧

IT HAS BEEN a month since I moved back into the house, and I am slowly healing. We were headed to Andy's funeral today. He passed away in his sleep this week with a smile on his face. I'm glad he came to peace with himself, and I was privileged to have known him.

"You look beautiful," Sebastian said as he walked up to me. We had been hanging out some. I didn't fully forgive him yet, and a serious relationship still scared me, but Sebastian was helping. If anything, he was being persistent. He was showing me how to open myself up again to new experiences. Sebastian and Andy had both sat me down and said being rich wasn't all bad. I didn't grow up rich, so I came in with a different mentality. I could use it for good. So I moved back into the house, and Sebastian made sure I always had fresh roses in my room. There was no proof that Isabella or her mom had anything to do with the bombing, but they dropped the lawsuit, so I wasn't going to go poking where I didn't need to be poking.

"That's quite a thing to say at a funeral."

"Can't you just take a compliment?"

"From you? I'm still getting used to them," I said as he leaned in for a kiss. He put his arm around me and we walked toward the car to join Mom and Jack. The rest of the family had no interest in attending. I watched the rows of pink plum blossoms pass by. They had just bloomed, and I felt the love Sir Anthony had put in planting all of them.

Some of us hung around sharing stories about Andy. Sebastian pulled me aside and showed me a letter. "This came in the mail today addressed to both of us. I've been waiting to read it with you."

Anne and Sebastian,

I hope you two have made up. If anything, I hope this letter brings you two physically together to talk out your differences. There is one more story I hadn't shared and I couldn't get myself to share with you in person. I bumped into the doctor that saw your Ai Po ten years after he treated her. We were on vacation. He was drunk and probably didn't know what he was saying or who I was. But he had something to share with me, and he told me that he never gave your Ai Po an abortion. I read through all your Ai Po's journals and never found any mention of her being pregnant or giving birth, but I assumed she was scared and did not want anyone in the family to find out she had birthed a son with Sir Anthony. I have to give Josephine props as she never mentioned anything either. It took me a long time, but I believe I have tracked him down. If this is the right guy, he's a grandfather now as well. You have an Uncle, Anne.

With much love,

Andy

"Why the hell would he tell us this now?!" Everyone went silent for a second and looked over at us. Sebastian pulled me outside and looked me in the eye.

"Anne, you have an uncle. A half-uncle, but another relative out there. You should be excited. Maybe he can shed some more light on your Ai Po."

"Maybe. Or maybe he's crazy. I won't think about it today. Today is Andy's day."

"That's right, it's Andy's day. I'll take you home afterward."

I looked at Sebastian with a big smile. "Home, I like the sound of that."

HISTORICAL DATES

1875: Page Act restricted the entry of Asian women who came for the purpose of prostitution. Enforcement of this Act was so restrictive it virtually stopped Chinese women from immigrating to the United States. This was the first restrictive federal immigration law in the United States.

1882: Chinese Exclusion Act. Ten year moratorium on Chinese labor immigration. Non-laborers had a hard time proving they were not laborers. Therefore, very few Chinese could enter the country. Chinese Americans not born in the United States were not permitted to become citizens, could not own property, and were barred from schools, jobs, and neighborhoods due to segregation.

1892: Geary Act extended the Chinese Exclusion Act for another ten years. In addition, each Chinese resident was required to register and obtain a certificate of residence. Without the certificate they could be deported.

1902: Chinese Exclusion Act extended for another ten years.

1904: Chinese Exclusion Act was made permanent.

1943: Magnuson Act repealed the Chinese Exclusion Act. Sentiments towards Chinese were changing for the better due to Chinese contributions in WWII. 105 Chinese immigrants were allowed in the United States each year and Chinese who were already in America could become naturalized citizens if they met requirements.

1945: WWII ends.

1948: Perez vs. Sharp. California Supreme Court ruled California's anti-miscegenation law unconstitutional. The last such ruling was from Ohio in 1887. California's ruling started a state-by-state campaign on repealing anti-miscegenation laws.

1965: Immigration and Nationality Act, effective July 1, 1968. The Act removed racial and national barriers. The immigrant quota was set to 170,000 immigrants per year from outside the Western Hemisphere, with a maximum of 20,000 from any one country.

1967: Loving vs Virginia. The U.S. Supreme Court ruled anti-miscegenation laws unconstitutional. Interracial marriages increased significantly after this. The last state constitution to be amended was in 2000.

ACKNOWLEDGMENTS

This book would not be in your hands if not for my awesome team of supporters.

First and foremost are Gordon and our two little ones who were there when I signed up for Self-Publishing School and had absolutely no idea what I was doing. They've watched me write, procrastinate, write, and procrastinate some more. You kids are the reason I am finally running after this dream. I love y'all so much and couldn't have done this without y'all.

To my parents and Mindy, the best sister ever, who were supportive when I quit my job to take care of the kids and then when I started writing a novel after years of education and technical work. Y'all have always been there for me, and I love y'all.

I cannot thank Qat Wanders enough for the time and energy she and her team spent on editing my book. She polished the book to where it is now without changing the essence of the story and answered my questions when I was completely lost. Thank you so much from the bottom of my heart.

Rob Williams of ILOVEMYCOVER was fantastic to work with and made a beautiful cover for my debut novel. Thank you so much.

Kimberly Miller, my accountabilitybuddy, has been waiting the longest for this book to come out and has been there every step of the way. Your weekly texts were filled with encouragement. I would have procrastinated much longer if not for you. Thank you.

I cannot say enough good things about the Self-Publishing School Fundamentals of Fiction group. Ramy Vance is the best coach a writer could ask for. In addition, he has brought a group of authors together who support and teach each other through the whole self-publishing process. This group is awesome.

My launch team, you have been amazing in giving your time and support for my first novel. I could not have launched my book without you. Thank you, thank you, thank you.

Last but not least, my writing club - Maureen Turner Carey, Jenne Turner, and Ellie Lin Ratliff - which started on a whim many years ago because we all wanted to write. I would never have continued my path towards where I am now if not for our monthly calls. To see y'all come up with stories made the writing real and kept the dream in the back of my mind instead of buried deep down. Thank you for always being there. I love you guys.

NEWSLETTER

To be the first to know about new book releases and other exclusive bonuses...

PLEASE REVIEW

Reviews go a long way in helping authors get the word out. Without them few would know about our books. Your review is one of a kind, and I can't thank you enough for your support.

Made in the USA
Middletown, DE
08 December 2018